Oh, she wanted she?

He was game.

After all, they had minutes left to live. Why not spend them thinking of enjoyable things?

"Well." He cleared his throat and straightened his back against the post, trying to get comfortable for this little round of sexting. Without the phones, of course. "I would definitely start out by taking you to my home in Sedona. It is a very cozy adobe atop a hill, looking out across red cliffs and miles of beautiful desert. And since there is an incredible sunset each night, where the sky bursts into hot pinks and blazing reds, I would set out a very nice bottle of wine and a blanket on my patio. We would watch the sunset and enjoy the majestic beauty of nature—"

"That sounds super romantic, but I don't know when my mother is coming to remove my head, so could you skip to the sex part, please?"

He grinned. "Okay, then, I would take you inside, remove your clothing. I would tell you that I was going to lick and kiss you from head to toe, but by the time I got done sucking one of your nipples and found your entrance wet and ready, I wouldn't be able to stop myself from pinning your hands over your head and taking you hard. Like a savage beast."

Fina bit her lower lip, her pupils dilating. "How hard?"

"You'd scream my name and claw at my back."

OTHER WORKS BY MIMI JEAN PAMFILOFF

COMING SOON!

The Librarian's Vampire Assistant
(Book 5) ← Finally! We get to hear directly from Miriam.

Fanged Love ← Your face is going to hurt from laughing.

The Dead King (King Series, Book 6) ← Can't wait! I need me some evil King!

THE ACCIDENTALLY YOURS SERIES

(Paranormal Romance/Humor)
Accidentally in Love with…a God? (Book 1)
Accidentally Married to…a Vampire? (Book 2)
Sun God Seeks…Surrogate? (Book 3)
Accidentally…Evil? (a Novella) (Book 3.5)
Vampires Need Not…Apply? (Book 4)
Accidentally…Cimil? (a Novella) (Book 4.5)
Accidentally…Over? (Series Finale) (Book 5)

THE BOYFRIEND COLLECTOR DUET

(New Adult/Suspense)
The Boyfriend Collector, Part 1
The Boyfriend Collector, Part 2

THE FATE BOOK DUET

(New Adult/Humor)
Fate Book
Fate Book Two

THE FUGLY DUET
(Contemporary Romance)
fugly
it's a fugly life

THE HAPPY PANTS SERIES
(Standalones/Romantic Comedy)
The Happy Pants Café (Prequel)
Tailored for Trouble (Book 1)
Leather Pants (Book 2)
Skinny Pants (Book 3)

IMMORTAL MATCHMAKERS, INC., SERIES
(Standalones/Paranormal/Humor)
The Immortal Matchmakers (Book 1)
Tommaso (Book 2)
God of Wine (Book 3)
The Goddess of Forgetfulness (Book 4)
Colel (Book 5)
Brutus (Book 6) ← You are here. ☺

THE KING SERIES
(Dark Fantasy/Suspense)
King's (Book 1)
King for a Day (Book 2)
King of Me (Book 3)
Mack (Book 4)
Ten Club (Book 5)

BRUTUS

The Immortal Matchmakers, Inc. Series
Book 6

MIMI JEAN PAMFILOFF

A Mimi Boutique Novel

Photographer: VJ Dunravan at Periodimages.com
Cover Design: Earthly Charms
Developmental Editing: Stephanie Elliot
Copyediting and Proof Reading: Pauline Nolet
Formatting: Paul Salvette

NOTE ABOUT BOOK PIRACY

"I'm not hurting anyone."

"I can't afford to buy books, so the author isn't losing money. I'd never buy them anyway."

"I don't think it's wrong. So many people do it."

"I bought the ebook. I own it. I can share it."

Wrong. Wrong. Wrong. And nope!

As an author who supports her family on this income, it's difficult to find the right words to convey how damaging illegal sharing and piracy is to me personally, to my fellow authors, and to the industry.

Bottom line, if a person buys a copy of a book or ebook, they do not now OWN the rights to that work. The author does. The reader has only purchased a right to that one, single copy.

In the case of paperbacks, that means a reader can share their copy with a friend, but they can't print off five hundred copies and give them out.

In the case of ebooks, it means the reader has purchased a license, granted by the author, for one person only. The reader can share their ereader. Sure. Okay! They can even share a book via licensed, tracked, and controlled share programs that the author has opted into (such as on Kindle). BUT if the reader decides to share any other way, that's making an illegal copy. That one illegal copy so innocently sent to friends or groups or posted on share sites can turn into hundreds, thousands, or millions.

Again, buying a book/ebook does not mean a reader now "owns" the book. They do not own distribution rights. They do not have the right to take an author's work and give it away to anyone as they see fit. Even libraries have special terms under which people can check out ebooks.

So please do not make illegal copies. Please do not share copies. Please do not download illegal copies.

As human beings, we all have a right to decide how we're compensated for our work and time. Strangers, the public, and book pirate sites don't have the right to decide for us.

As for these sites that claim they're not doing anything wrong? The sites pirated book lovers go to and think they're not hurting anyone? What sort of person would put up a website that uses stolen work (or encourages its users to share stolen work) in order to make money for themselves, either through website traffic or direct sales? **Haven't you ever wondered?** Putting up thousands of pirated books onto a website or creating those anonymous ebook file-sharing sites takes time and resources. Quite a lot, actually.

So who are these people? Do you think they're decent, ethical people with good intentions? Why do they set up camp anonymously in countries—

Russia and Iran, for example—where they can't be touched?

And the money they make from advertising every time you go to their website, or through selling stolen work, **what are they using it for? The answer is you don't know.** They could be terrorists, organized criminals, or just greedy bastards. But one thing we DO know is that **THEY ARE CRIMINALS** who don't care about you, your family, or me and mine. **And their intentions can't be good.**

And every time someone illegally shares or downloads a book from one of these sites, **THEY ARE BREAKING the law** and HELPING these people BREAK THE LAW.

Meanwhile, people like me, who work to support a family and children, are left wondering why anyone would condone this. Assholes, I guess.

And for those who legally purchased/borrowed/obtained my work from a reputable retailer (not sure, just ask me!) muchas thank yous! You rock.

DEDICATION

To Trenna Harris.
You loved to smile and have adventures.
So this one is for you, girl.
You will be missed.

WARNING

This book contains a smokin' hot immortal warrior looking for his forever love, a randy invisible unicorn, and bad, bad, *such* bad language. Okay, and some sex. Fine, yes! Lots of sex! And a kitten, a bit of violence, a man who loves knitting, *mannibalism,* unruly deities, Mayan priests who babysit animals, a naked goddess who wears a bee bikini, leather pants (for men), a very randy ghost who's desperate for her HEA, anecdotes about evil mermen, a BIG plot twist even the author didn't see coming, and a ton of romancy kind of stuff.

BRUTUS

CHAPTER ONE

"No. No more. I beg of you…" Tethered to a large tree, his hands bound together behind his back, Brutus, the world's most fearless immortal warrior, was finally at his breaking point. His shoulder blades were raw from the friction of the bark, and his cock literally felt like it might fall off. Also, there were dried twigs and leaves up his ass crack. He hated sitting naked in the dirt, especially in such a dense, dark jungle. Things lived in the dirt. Scary things.

Nothing as scary as these women.

"Silence, male," the tall blonde Amazonian woman growled and removed her suede sarong, leaving her completely nude with her pert nipples pointing straight at him like two predatory eyes. "Get that thing hard for me. Chop-chop. I've been waiting all morning for my turn."

I cannot possibly come another time. It wasn't that these females weren't attractive, with their tall lean bodies and tanned skin, but they were rough. They were demanding. And frankly, he was not okay with being bossed around like this.

He was the one who gave orders.

He was a leader in the gods' army.

He was a legendary immortal warrior.

And idiot me came alone on this important mission. Now he was a sex prisoner. Well, sorta.

Truth was, he could probably break free if he wanted, but then these women would likely try to kill him, and he'd have to fight his way out of the jungle. Sure, he'd win—no woman was a match for his massive muscles and experience in battle—but he would lose the war. The war that would end everything. These women could mean the difference between winning and losing.

Brutus tilted his head back and rested it on the tree behind him. "You're not getting what you want. I'm spent. I'm tired and hungry. So kill me if you must, but I'm done." He knew they wouldn't really harm him. They were much too horny, and from the looks of things, not one man among them.

The female warrior crouched in front of him and squeezed his unshaved face, digging her dagger-like nails into the skin. "I want sex," she snarled, "and you shall give it to me or…" She whipped out a long blade, just as the previous ninety-seven women had.

He flinched, feeling the sharp edge of the knife pressing against his right testicle. "Hurry. Get it over with, then," he said, his tone pure cockiness.

"Helga! Leave him alone," a familiar female voice barked. "Can't you see the man is exhausted? He'll be no use to us if you cut the coconuts off his tree, and my mother will be displeased."

Helga slowly stood, taking her blade with her. "Stay out of this, Fina. It is my turn with the man, and I say whether he lives or dies. At the moment, I say *die*."

Wearing a bikini made of animal hides, Fina stepped into view, appearing between two tall mango trees. She was by far the best looking among their tribe, with her wide hips, toned arms and legs, and almond-shaped eyes. Her most striking feature, however, was the unusual gold streak on her right temple that contrasted her long dark hair. Her mouth, on the other hand, left something to be desired. *Very mean scowl.*

Fina was the one who had initially encountered him in the jungle. *What luck!* he'd thought. His mission to find this group was a matter of the utmost importance, but instead of hearing him out, Fina had hit him over the head. He'd woken up here with his hands tied behind his back and his torso roped to this tree.

It had been over a week now, and his attempts to tell them why he'd come were futile. It was as if they tuned him out or had very selective hearing when it came to male voices. Not that he was much of a talker. It was a well-known fact back home that he and his men, all human warriors who'd been gifted the immortal light of the gods (making them demigods), had developed a bond so strong that they could communicate telepathically. Years of practice.

"Helga, I do not wish to quarrel over this *man*," Fina said, placing a sour note on the word *man*—like he was a useless piece of shit or a rotten banana. "I am merely pointing out that we have not seen a male around here in decades, and such a fine, well-equipped specimen at that. If you kill him, the others will be very upset. They've already planned out a sex schedule for the next six months."

Six months? "No. That's fine," Brutus interjected. "She's free to kill me. I've lived long enough."

Both women looked at him. Fina growled. Helga smiled with sadistic delight.

No, he didn't truly have a death wish, but Brutus had been growing tired of his role, heading off one apocalypse after another—the invasion of evil Mayan priests, the invasion of evil vampires, the invasion of evil vampire Mayan priests. And now? The immortal plague. It was all so repetitive, and, frankly, it took the joy out of winning. *Disaster. Triumph. Disaster. Triumph.*

Of course, the winning streak only applied to his career. The relationship front was a whole other story: *Disaster. Bigger disaster.* For example, he had never wanted a mate. He'd never asked for one. Yet the Universe, in her infinite sadistic wisdom, had insisted on mating him to a goddess named Colel. Most called her "Bees" on account of her being the Mistress of Bees, who wore an enormous immortal beehive on her head—very sexy. He liked a woman who cared for the tinier creatures of the world. However, Colel had been given two mates. Two! Practically unheard of. Needless to say, the other male won. Some demigod-slash-vampire florist asshole, named after an orchid, who couldn't save the world if he tried.

Unlike me. Brutus had rescued the world hundreds of times.

Now that things were over with the goddess, he'd lost all taste for women. No, no. He wasn't into men either. Unicorns were a hard no, too. Sex fairies were okay on special occasions, like when Cimil, the Goddess of the Underworld, threw one of her famous barbecues or naked knitting parties— he loved to knit. For animals. Particularly his elderly cocker spaniel, Niccolo. The point was, after having his heart broken, the Universe thought it would be hysterical to set him on a course that had led him here. To *this* jungle. During a time in his life when he wanted nothing to do with women.

And there are so many of them. Eesh…

"Listen, ladies." He cleared his throat and puffed out his large chest, determined to finally be heard. "I have been a good sport and sat here patiently for over a week, being ridden like a merry-go-round pony, but now it is time for you to allow me to complete my mission. Because, frankly, we're out of time, and this cow," he glanced at his cock, "has no more milk."

"Cow?" Fina chuckled. "That's a funny thing to

call your manhood."

Helga started laughing, too. "He compared himself to a cow. He thinks he's valuable."

The two women doubled over, cracking up.

Brutus growled. They really were man-haters. "Are you going to let me talk to your leader or not?" he asked Fina. Several times she'd referred to her mother, who he assumed was their leader.

Fina looked down at him, her dark eyes shimmering as speckles of sunlight filtered through the tree canopy and danced across her face. Like the other women, she had dark skin, high cheekbones, and full juicy lips, but something about her felt different. Perhaps it was the defiant gleam in her eye. He wasn't sure. He simply knew she was the only woman he hadn't had sex with. Well, her and her mother—the leader whom he'd yet to meet.

"You owe me," he added, hoping to persuade her. "I demand an audience with your leader."

"How do I owe you? You are our prisoner." Fina laughed again, and this time, it got under his skin.

"I saved your cat." He'd come across the tiny kitten stuck in a tree while hiking through the jungle in search of these women. That was how Fina had managed to sneak up on him.

"I was teaching Zeus to hunt, as any good cat should know how to do. *You* interrupted us."

"Hunt? In the jungle? It's a house cat." And where Fina had gotten a hold of one this far into the

Amazon rainforest was anyone's guess.

"It's a warrior. Like me." Her pink little lips made an angry pucker.

He chuckled, pleased to finally get a reaction from her that wasn't laughter. "Love, you are no warrior. And trust me, I know—"

Before he could complete his sentence, Fina spit in her hand, crouched, and took his manhood in her palm. He felt his entire body recoil with fear and then…

Brutus groaned, falling into a state of quivers and ecstasy radiating from the tip of his cock, down the shaft, and out through his torso and limbs. *Oh gods. Oh gods. What is she doing to me?* He was at her mercy. Every ounce of his determination to complete his mission melted away beneath the expert strokes of her rough, strong, but petite little hand.

He clenched his eyes shut and made fists behind his back. *I'm going to co—*

"Oh, look. You're all fixed now." She smiled devilishly and withdrew her hand.

Brutus looked down to see all ten inches of "the General" standing at attention. "Don't stop. Don't sto—"

"He's all yours, Helga." Fina stood, turned, and disappeared into the jungle with a proud spring in her step. The echo of her laughter faded off in the distance.

He winced, looking up into Helga's hungry gaze. *Jesus, no.*

"Well, well, I guess the man cow is ready for another milking." Helga straddled his lap. "Now get moving and give me pleasure. I will stay here all night if I must."

Dear gods. He'd better get this over with as quickly as possible. Perhaps they'd allow him one night of sleep. Just one. Then, tomorrow, he could figure out a new plan, including how to persuade Fina to give him an audience with her mother.

CHAPTER TWO

Zac, God of Temptation and the tiredest motherfucker on the planet, stood chained to a boulder in the world's sparkliest cave, wondering how his existence had led him to this perplexingly bleak moment: *Unicorn prisoner.*

It seemed the Universe was on a crash course for revenge, repeatedly handing him one clusterfuck of a situation after another. Did the Universe have a bone to pick with him? All men? All incredibly handsome immortal men?

He didn't know, but being a god, he sensed something in the air. A woman-scorned vibe.

Maybe that's just the randy evil unicorn trying to give me a blowjob. He glanced down at two fiery eyes bobbing over his groin. Yep. Just two hovering eyes. The rest was invisible.

"Sorry, Minky, but it's not going to work. You don't even have a body, and if you did, my heart belongs to Tula. It will always belong to Tula." Tula was the prim-and-proper assistant at their office, Immortal Matchmakers, Inc., where they were tasked with finding mates for even the most unlovable of immortals. Tula—a human—was unlike any being Zac had ever met, her heart made of pure goodness. So good, in fact, that every effort to tempt her—as was his role since he *was* the God of Temptation—into his arms had failed horribly. Total disaster. It wasn't until he opened his heart to Tula for the right reason, love, that she finally gave in. It was the moment he realized she was his mate and the moment when the Universe began doing everything in her power to keep them apart.

Which was how he ended up here. Locked inside Minky's private lair.

Minky growled out a string of mumbled words.

"Hey, don't blame me," he said. "It was your plan to trick me into being your man. And might I remind you, Minky, you were perfectly aware of my affections for Tula at the time. What were you thinking anyway, huh?" He had been trying to bring Tula back from…from…well, he wasn't exactly sure. Tula had died during a very unfortunate boating incident, and not long after, her ghost began appearing to him and only him. But knowing that her spirit had not moved on from this world had convinced him he could bring her back. All he needed was her body. *Her perfectly preserved body.*

The problem was that an insane, horny, evil unicorn was in possession of said body. Minky ate it.

Which was how he'd become Minky's sex pet. Minky had claimed she could reunite Tula's spirit with her unicorn-preserved physical form. For a price. So, eager to be with the woman he loved, Zac had agreed blindly, unaware of the cost: Minky wanted him for herself. And, as anyone will tell you, a deal struck with a unicorn is unbreakable. *Sneaky, dirty fucking unicorn! I will never love you!*

Hovering over him, Minky rumbled and released a plume of fire.

"Yeah, well, too bad!" he barked. "I guess neither of us gets what we want, then. Oh, and by the way? You reneged on our deal. You were supposed to help get Tula back in her body, so I don't feel one little crumb of remorse."

Minky grumbled something about never specifically saying that she would help with that. She'd merely said she knew who could: Cimil, Goddess of the Underworld. Unfortunately, Cimil had been locked up by some very angry mermen. And by locked up, he meant that Cimil'd been thrown to the bottom of the ocean inside a barrel. Minky had said she knew how to get to Cimil; she'd said she could *help* him.

And now she claims otherwise? "That's cheating. You know the agreement was to help bring Tula back. But you know what? That's fine. Because…because…" He tried to imagine some sort of threat that would make Minky see how ridiculous this whole thing was. "Even if you try to set me free, I will refuse to leave you. Uh-huh." He bobbed his head. "That's right, Minky. A deal's a deal! You wanted me and now you have me. Forever! Let's see how you like being mated to a god who will never want you!"

Grumble, grumble.

He shrugged. "Nope. Sorry. No take-backs, Minky. You're stuck with a man who hates your sparkly guts!"

Grumble, grumble.

"Well, you should have thought about that before. Tula still roams the earth as a spirit, and *you* still have her body. Yet here I am. Tied up in your rainbow-colored turd cave. I'd say that makes you a very evil unicorn—one I will never love or have sex with, so I hope you're into squishy, flaccid bananas."

Minky's red eyes turned into swirly blue orbs of sadness and then faded, leaving him alone in the cave.

"Hey! Where the hell do you think you're going, huh? Get back here!" Zac yelled. "Look at my limp, but very large, manhood. It's like a flag on a windless afternoon! A deflated party balloon! A floppy garden hose! All for you, Minky! In your honor." Zac waited for a response to his taunts, but the unicorn was gone.

Dammit, Minky. He needed to push her buttons so that she might stab him with her unihorn. He could not die, not in the human sense, but if his human form was destroyed, his spirit would be sent back to his realm. From there, he could attempt to contact one of his thirteen brethren—who likely had no clue he'd been taken—or he could take another trip through the portal and gain a new humanlike body. Either way, he'd be free of Minky and able to seek help. Someone had to know how to make this beast give up Tula's sweet, petite little body.

"Minky! You evil fuck! Get back here!"

CHAPTER THREE

Sedona, Arizona.

"Has anyone heard from Brutus?" Votan, God of Death and War, sat at the head of the long rectangular table in the great meeting hall of the gods' newly renovated headquarters that also served as a military base for their human army. Yes, human. It was a well-known fact that fourteen gods could hardly keep an eye on billions of people; therefore, they recruited people to join the Uchben (their official name) to serve as their eyes and ears—teachers, lawyers, doctors, soldiers. To be an Uchben was a great honor and came with wonderful medical benefits. Also, a 401k. And those who proved themselves invaluable were given something even more valuable: the light of the gods. Immortality.

Brutus was one such man, soon to be promoted and in command of the god's Uchben army. His current boss, Gabrán—a very cantankerous, very ancient Scot—was set to retire. Everyone knew that Brutus secretly looked up to the man and thought of him like a father. He'd taught Brutus everything he knew about leading battles, sword fighting, and killing Maaskab, those evil Mayan priests. But Gabrán had finally had enough of apocalypses and planned to rebuild his family's castle and raise pumpkins.

Maybe my family and I should join him. Votan, too, had grown weary of fighting wars. Honestly, he would rather spend his days with his wife and children. Teaching them about war. Telling stories about war. Watching movies about war. Basically, anything having to do with war except for fighting in them.

Votan looked around the room at the faces of his brethren. Each sat around the stone table carved with intricate symbols depicting the individual gods and their multitude of individual powers: war, happiness, time travel, sunshine, love, fertility, drumming, math, garage sale hunting, decoupage— you name it, one of the gods had a power for it.

However, only ten of the fourteen deities were present at the moment. Zac, God of Temptation, was missing, and three others were locked up—the Goddess of Fertility, the God of Eclipses, and K'ak. No one really knew what K'ak did, so no title for him. *And no freedom.* As of today, all unmated immortals were to be confined due to a plague that only affected them. Luckily for everyone, the recent renovations here in Sedona included a brand-new, very large prison. And expanded spa, bowling alley, underground shopping mall, and a food court.

Stupid! But most of the ladies, including Votan's wife, had insisted that building a prison and command center alone would only serve his "pigheaded, male ego" that lived for war. Their soldiers needed entertainment and downtime, too.

Ha. Well, who's pigheaded now? The brand-new prison was the only thing keeping humans safe. Something was causing unmated immortals to "flip," turning them into evil killers. Sort of like in those human zombie movies, except this disease had a cure: being mated. Or was it love? *It's kind of romantic, really.*

Votan shuddered at having such a mushy, unmanly thought.

"No. No word from Brutus," said Belch, the God of Wine and Decapitation. Belch's true name was Acan, but since he'd spent tens of thousands of years pantsless and drunk, the Belch name kind of stuck. Now he spent his days sober and with his mate, Margarita, who ran a chain of fitness clubs. And he wore pants. Also, he looked pretty damned good. Gone was the giant beer belly, replaced with the muscles of a warrior.

As it should be. The gods were meant to be worshipped—beautiful, tall, exotic. Yes, some had black hair, like he did. Some had golden locks. But they all had varying hues of tanned skin. They were an amalgamation of every race, so that when a human gazed upon them, they saw something of themselves reflected back. *Except much hotter, of course.* They were deities, after all. Thus the turquoise eyes—a telltale sign of their immortality.

"So, brother, what is the plan?" Belch asked. "Do we send a team after Brutus? Do we focus on the singles mixer in the prison?"

"No," interjected Chaam, the God of Male Virility, who sat opposite Votan at the end of the long table. As brothers, they looked much alike, with long blue-black hair, their height measuring almost seven feet. "We must use our resources to round up the single immortals first—especially the vampires, who pose the biggest threat to humans. Then we worry about finding mates for them."

Votan rubbed his forehead with worry. The gods had fought many wars throughout the centuries, but never anything like this. *How does one fight an enemy who is temporarily evil?* Those who were flipping to the evil side were their brothers and sisters of the immortal world. They could be cured by simply finding love. *Easier said than done.*

Bottom line, the immortal community—vampires, demigods, incubi, mermen, and all the rest—was predominantly male. That included their immortal soldiers. Add it all together, and they needed to find women. Fast.

Brutus had been tasked with locating a tribe of female warriors rumored to live deep in the Amazon jungle. Nevertheless, even if Brutus succeeded in bringing them back, one hundred females weren't enough. *And that's assuming they choose mates from our very fine selection of rabid, incarcerated men.*

The Goddess of Forgetfulness, aka "Forgetty," was helping by entering all the singles into a giant immortal dating website that their brother Zac was supposed to be curating. Unfortunately, Zac had disappeared, likely grieving over the loss of his human mate, Tula. *Such a shame.* Tula had been a truly good person. In any case, the website was proving too slow, and dozens of immortals were flipping every minute. Simply put, they were out of time.

"I should not have sent Brutus on such an important mission alone," Votan mumbled. "The only choice we have is to do as Chaam suggests and shift our limited resources to rounding up the rest of the unmated immortals. Hopefully before they have flipped, to lessen our casualties." Votan sighed with grief, knowing they had but a few hundred mated couples among tens of thousands of singles, and very few on their side were trained soldiers. "I'm sorry. I wish I had another solution."

"Do not despair, brother," said Colel, the Mistress of Bees—a blonde, statuesque goddess who wore a white silk toga and her trademark beehive hat. "You are doing your very best, and azzz you know, we are quite lazy when it comes to war, so our expectations are super low." Everyone around the table muttered in agreement. "But perhaps you are right. Brutus should not have gone alone. I will take my soldiers and track him down." One of her "soldiers" flew from the hole in her hat and started buzzing around her face. "Stop it, Chuck! I know you're supposed to bee on vacation, but this izzz important!"

Votan resisted rolling his eyes. As God of War (and Death) it was his job to lead during such calamitous times, but trying to orchestrate a simple meeting with his brethren felt like herding leprechauns—basically a circus comprised of very small-minded beings who were easily distracted by anything shiny. "We cannot spare you, Colel. We need every mated deity helping with the roundup. Even if some of our soldiers have been given immortality, they can still be killed. *You* cannot." If a deity's body was destroyed, they simply went and got another. Everyone else—vampires, demigods, and were-penguins alike—died if their bodies were destroyed.

"But I worry something has happened to Brutus," Colel argued, swatting at that bee, who continued buzzing angrily in her face.

"Brutus can handle himself, sister," said Votan. "Do not fret."

Colel frowned. "But, brother, I really think—"

"No. You will not go after him. And I'm certain your chosen mate would agree." Brutus was actually Colel's mate, but so was Rys, the florist. It was highly unusual for the Universe to offer two males to one female, but these days, anything was possible. The Universe was off her rocker, doing all sorts of crazy things. Though humans remained unaware, subconsciously they had begun behaving erratically, too—hoarding toilet paper and locking themselves indoors for months at a time. *Very strange behavior. It is as if they think they're the ones with the plague.*

In any case, things would only get worse until this disaster ended. As for Colel, she had chosen Rys over Brutus. It broke the poor chap's heart, which was one more reason Votan did not want Colel traipsing after the man. Brutus was likely some-where in the jungle, getting Colel out of his system with a hundred very randy, cock-starved females.

Votan sighed. *I bet he's having the time of his life… Wish I'd gone with him.* Not that he'd ever be unfaithful to his wife, Emma, but the frequent sex in their relationship had been replaced by parenting. They never got time alone, and when they were together, Emma was too tired. Now he relied entirely on fantasies to get by. Yes, porn. *And to be ravaged by such strong, savage women.* "Mmmm…"

"Votan! Really? Are you getting a boner right in the middle of our meeting?" Colel barked. "I swear—you and your lust for war never cease to amazzze me."

Votan cleared his throat and glanced down at the tent in his black leather pants. "I was-I was…yes. Getting a war boner," he lied. "Now may we get on with our important meeting?"

"Is it important? Really?" Cimil, the Goddess of the Underworld, cackled from the back of the room in her fold-out chair. She was the only one not seated at the table. Mostly because everyone was pissed at her, but also because she said the table clashed with her outfit. At present, she had a huge pregnant belly and was wearing a Hefty bag with a red bow that matched her flaming red hair. Very unusual outfit, even for her. But no one asked because no one cared. *Just Cimil being Cimil.*

"I think you're all spinning your wheels," Cimil added.

"What is that supposed to mean?" griped Votan.

"Only that you all think you're in control. You *think* you have a say in how this story ends." She cackled again.

"Cimiiil," growled Votan, "if you are keeping something from us—"

"Nope. Nope. Not me." Cimil began twiddling her fingers.

Belch stepped in. "Sister, please. If you have information that could help us stop the plague affecting thousands of immortals and prevent millions of humans from dying by their hands, then you have to tell us. My mate is human. Her daughter is human. I do not want anything to happen to them."

Cimil clamped her red lips shut and stared blankly. Whatever she knew, Cimil wasn't about to share it.

This calls for some threats. Luckily, as God of Death and War, Votan was skilled at such things.

"Tell us what you know, Cimil, or we'll call you-know-who," he warned.

"Who?" asked Cimil, clapping excitedly. "Please say naked clowns."

Votan rolled his eyes. "The mermen." The mermen hated Cimil with a passion and were still unaware that she had gotten free from her watery prison at the bottom of the ocean. Considering that they'd put her there as punishment for orchestrating the death of several of their men, they would not be happy when they found out.

"Nice try, brother," Cimil threw back. "We all know the mermen have their flippers full at present. Their unmated members have turned evil, too."

It was true. Roen, their leader, was doing his best to round them up unharmed with hopes that the gods would soon find a cure. "Maybe so, but trust me when I say, sister, that if they found out you were free, they would take every captured evil merman and set them on your doorstep. Not even your children could fight them off." And Cimil's four children were probably the most vicious, heartless creatures on the planet. He couldn't imagine how terrible this next batch would be.

Cimil stuck out her tongue. "You're all about as much fun as an ingrown toenail. And may I remind you that if the mermen discover I am free, they will not only seek to destroy me, but declare war on all the gods once this whole *fiesta* of *violencia* is *finito*."

"Yes," Votan growled. "And they will lose. Then

you will be responsible for their extinction, so I recommend, for once in your sorry abomination of an existence, that you play nice and use your powers for good." He exhaled with a grunt. "Now, use your gifts and tell us what you know!"

As Goddess of the Underworld, Cimil could speak to the dead, who resided on another plane where time ceased to exist. The dead from the past and future mingled in one enormous party until they either moved on to rejoin the Universe's cosmic soup or they decided to return for another ride on the merry-go-round of life. Cimil's power gave her the ability to listen to the billions of voices and filter that noise to form a picture of the future. *Or was it the past? Because to the dead of the future, the here and now was the past? So confusing.*

Cimil leaned back in her chair and made little circles over her enormous belly. "Here's the thing. I *have* been trying to use my powers, but the dead aren't making any sense. I think my increased hormone levels are interfering. That, or I have gas. Or they're all mad at me, too—I kinda cleaned them out during poker the other ni—"

"Cimil! *What* did you hear? What are they saying?" asked Votan.

"I keep hearing them say, 'The beginning is the end.'" Cimil shrugged.

"Isn't the saying supposed to be, 'The end is just another beginning'?" Votan asked.

"Yes. That's why it think my little dumplings

are making my signals wonky. And then, last night, I had some of the dead over for stripe poker and—"

"You mean strip poker?" Colel inquired.

"No. *Stripe* poker. You play with a zebra, and every time you lose a hand, the zebra must remove a stripe."

Everyone, including Votan, blinked at Cimil.

"What? Haven't you played before?" Cimil asked, sounding shocked.

"No. Absolutely not," Votan stated.

"Your loss. Anyway, there I was, winning my fourth hand, my zebra up ten stripes, when all of a sudden, the dead started screaming."

"What were they saying?" Belch asked, leaning forward in his leather exec chair.

Cimil's voice got quiet. "Twinkies."

Votan frowned. "Twinkies? They said Twinkies?"

"No. I'm hungry. Got any Twinkies?" Cimil got up from her chair and walked out of the room.

No one said a word.

After several moments, Votan pushed back in his chair. "Well, that was predictably fruitless." All she did was throw kerosene on an already confusing bonfire of challenges. To sum it all up: They had an immortal plague that was a threat to billions of mortals, Zac was nowhere to be found, no one had heard a peep from Brutus, the mermen were going to lose their shit when they found out Cimil was free, humans were going nutso, and, on top of all that, the dead were freaking out, but they didn't know why.

What else could possibly go wrong?

CHAPTER FOUR

By the time the sun rose the next morning, Brutus had finally made up his mind. He was through with being the polite houseguest. Jungle guest. Whatever. He had hoped if he allowed these females to work off a little steam, he might gain their respect. Or at least a little goodwill.

Negative. He would have to treat these women as hostile forces, meaning they would do as he said, or he would kill them. *Kidding.* He might enjoying giving them a good spanking if the opportunity ever arose. *They are so rude and uncivilized.* And this coming from an Uchben warrior. Uchben was the official name for the members of the gods' army, himself being the toughest beast of the lot. But even he and his elite squad of soldiers possessed *some* manners. It was becoming abundantly clear that no man could quell these females' aggressive, randy dispositions.

"Time to go and find the chief." And some clothes. He pulled on the rope tethering him to the tree. Nothing happened.

What the devil? He tugged again, this time giving it all his might. "Arrrrgh!" The rope dug into his chest and wrists. *Dammit all to hell.* The rope was made of something very strong.

He groaned. *Why am I surprised?* These women were a tribe of immortal warriors. Of course they would have rope of superior strength. *Still, I must tryyyy...* He pulled again, putting everything he had into it.

"You can't break free. You know that, right?" Fina appeared out of nowhere, holding her white and brown striped kitten, stroking its soft little ears.

"Release me at once!" Brutus growled in her general direction.

"Why would I do that?"

"Because, as I already told you and your band of cum bandits, I am here on official business. From the gods. I need to deliver a message to your leader."

She narrowed her eyes and stopped stroking her cat. "Did you just call us cum bandits?"

"If it talks like a cum bandit and walks like a cum ba—"

"I beg your pardon! We are great warriors. We take what is ours because it is our right. We are *not* thieves."

Oh. Had he hit a nerve? "The General says otherwise."

"Who?"

"The General." He glanced down at his flaccid member.

She shook her head and tsked with pity. "Well, looks pretty weak and sad for such a title."

Brutus glared. "You try having sex with almost a hundred women nonstop for a week."

She toggled her head. "Not my cup of tea."

Cup of tea? That was an oddly civilized phrase for a woman cut off from the world. "Where were you educated?" he asked.

"Why do you ask?"

"Well, you speak like a modern human, and now that I'm listening to your accent, you sound like you might be from the east coast."

"Boston. I went to boarding school in Boston, and then I later completed my BA in world history at Harvard. Mother insisted I learn the ways of the outside world."

Impressive. "Do all of the women here go to school outside?"

"Just me." She raised her chin. "I am to be leader someday."

"Ah. I see. Well, then if you attended classes in Boston, you might be aware of the state of chaos in the human world."

She shrugged. "I noticed nothing out of the ordinary."

"How long has it been since you returned home to this jungle?"

"Hmmm...not sure exactly. We're not big on calendars around here."

"So you don't know how old you are?" he asked.

"Three hundred—I think? To be honest, we're not too big on birthdays either."

"Well, if you truly are three centuries old, you look phenomenal," Brutus said, hoping to butter her up a little.

"Thank you." She dipped her head of long dark hair, the golden streak catching the sunlight, as if she were a magical creature.

Perhaps she is. "Might I ask how your tribe became immortal?"

"Who knows? My mother is the oldest at six hundred years old, and she doesn't know."

Very interesting. He wondered what their gene pool was comprised of and if they would be compatible with any of his men—some were demigods now after being gifted the light of the gods, like himself. Those were the ones they had to worry about. The plain old human soldiers were fine.

"Well, Fina, I suggest if you care for your mother and your people that you allow me to—"

Suddenly, the kitten jumped from her arms and ran over to him, brushing his little furry face on the soles of his feet.

"Zeus! What are you doing? Get away from that despicable male!" She crouched and tried to grab the kitten, but it darted straight up his leg and chest and up into the tree.

Brutus chuckled. "Looks like I'm not the only one who grows tired of your attitude."

She ignored him and called to the cat. "Zeus! Kitty, kitty. Please come down."

"I'm sure you have nothing to worry about.

Since getting stuck in trees is part of your training process." He chuckled. "Can't wait to see him go up against a jaguar."

"Shut up," she snarled and turned her attention back to the cat. "Zeus! Baby kitty. Please come down! I'll give you some nice snake meat."

"I'm afraid you'll have to climb up there and get him."

"I can't," she huffed.

"Why not?"

"I'm afraid of heights."

Brutus refrained from laughing. What sort of warrior feared heights? However, now was not the time to foster any ill will. "I will rescue your cat if you agree to give me an audience with your mother."

Fina frowned at him. "Nice try." She turned to leave.

"Where are you going?"

"To fetch Helga. She loves climbing trees."

Oh no. Not Helga. She would want more sex! "By the time you get there and back, your fur ball will have become a nice snack for a python or bigger cat. Sadly, I won't be able to rescue him."

"There are no pythons in this part of the jungle, and we haven't seen a jaguar in decades."

Hmmph! "All right. Then a poisonous snake!"

She kept marching away toward a dense patch of banana trees. Clearly, she was a woman who did not respond to fear. If he weren't tied to a tree, he'd find that extremely sexy. "Then let me go because you do not want to watch your entire tribe slaughtered. Because, trust me, they will be!"

Fina stopped and turned to face him. "No one can best us in battle. Not even with guns. Note how we have successfully fended off invaders for centuries."

"I'm not speaking of invaders," he warned. "I'm speaking of the plague that is turning immortals against one another. It is only a question of time before the illness reaches here. You say you and your people are undefeated, but when they turn and start killing each other, you will be helpless to stop it. Or perhaps you will join them."

She narrowed her dark eyes. "You lie. This is a ploy to get me to untie you."

"Fina, I am an Uchben soldier and next in line to lead the gods' army. Do you honestly believe I would take my time to come here and warn you if it were untrue? I have much better things to do: rogue immortals to hunt and humans to babysit so that they don't blow up this planet and take us all with them. Also, I have an elderly cocker spaniel waiting for me at home. Men like me do not abandon their needy pets without good cause. My purpose for coming was to warn you," he lied. His purpose was to convince them to return to Sedona for a singles mixer and hopefully some weddings.

He suddenly wondered whom Fina would choose should he succeed.

She stared for a moment, worrying her bottom lip. He could see the wheels turning in her head. "How did you come to find out about us?" she asked.

"The Mistress of Bees, Colel, said she encountered your tribe while tending to her flock."

"You mean the crazy lady who wears a living hive on her head?"

He nodded. "That would be the one." Or "bee" the one? Who knew. "And of course, Cimil, Goddess of the Underworld, agreed that I should make this journey."

Fina's mouth fell open. "Did you say Cimil?"

"Yes."

"The one who rides the invisible beast that breathes fire from its nostrils and can incinerate a man in three seconds?" Fina spoke excitedly, as if they were discussing her favorite rock star.

"Yes. That would be Minky, her insane vampire unicorn."

"I have to tell Mother." Fina turned to leave again. She looked like she was terrified.

"Wait! Where are you going? What about your kitten?"

Fina turned and darted back. "Oh crap. I forgot." She went behind the tree, and within a few seconds, Brutus was loose.

Brutus stretched his sore arms. "Ahhh…that feels incredible."

"Hurry! Hurry up. There is no time to waste."

Fina began tugging on his hand. "Get Zeus, and let's go."

Brutus felt a sharp tingly sensation spike up his arm, radiating from where her hand touched his. *What is that?* Like before, when she'd touched his "spear of delight," it felt incredible. Amazing even.

He got to his feet and blinked down at her, feeling his heart thumping away inside his chest. He wondered what magical powers this warrior princess might possess.

"Wake up!" She slapped him.

"Ow! Why did you hit me?" He covered his stinging cheek.

"You seemed entranced or something." She started pushing him toward the tree. "Chop-chop! Get the kitty."

The hitting was very rude. He was a seasoned soldier and could take all sorts of pain, but he hated bad manners.

"Turn away," he commanded.

"Why?" she asked.

"Because I am unclothed."

She laughed. "Are you getting shy all of a sudden?"

He shrugged. "Maybe." He'd never climbed a tree with his nuts hanging out.

"Fine." She turned, but when he got up to the first branch, he caught her looking.

He almost said something, but the look in her dark eyes made him take notice. Was that a spark of lust? Perhaps the spark he felt, albeit unusual, was mutual.

Strange to feel something so soon after losing Colel. Perhaps all this hanky-panky was messing with his head.

CHAPTER FIVE

Brutus thought that Fina's village looked like something out of a fantastic dream, with the dwellings built into the green-and-black cliffs, and tiers of towering bamboo ladders scaling hundreds of feet off the ground. A ten-story-high iridescent-turquoise waterfall spilled down the center of the cliff, directly between the rustic dwellings.

"Great Waterfall of Manacapuru," he muttered. He'd heard legends of it over the years, but no one had ever seen it in person. *It's even more beautiful than I imagined.*

The waterfall emptied into a wide lagoon with two sandy white beaches on either side. At the far end, where the mouth of the lagoon flowed out into a small river, a wooden bridge connected the beaches, where groups of women either practiced their swordsmanship or sat under an open-aired thatched-roof structure, drinking, eating, and grilling meats over an open pit.

Food. Swords. Warrior women. I'm in heaven.

"This is beautiful," he said, staring at a group of topless women wrestling in the sand.

"Keep marching." Fina pushed him from behind while he held the kitten.

Almost immediately, heads began turning, and it became instantly clear that he might be mistaken about this being paradise. He resisted the urge to press Zeus over his groin as an act of modesty.

Who am I kidding? I've had sex with everyone here. Everyone except Fina and her mother.

Not that he wanted to. He hadn't even enjoyed his time with the others, the acts feeling completely mechanical even when he came. *Like scratching a tickle in my nose.* He would hardly call it climaxing.

Helga was the first to break away from the crowd under the thatched roof to their right. "Fina! What is the meaning of this? No man is allowed inside our village." She drew her long hunting knife from the sheath strapped to her side.

"Put a fig in it, Helga, or I'll have you walk the coals tonight." Fina pushed Brutus from behind once more. "Keep moving, big man."

Helga snarled, but proceeded no farther. The other women held their fierce, dark gazes on him. Some even yelped, like they were terrified by his presence.

What am I missing?

Fina brought him to one of the few huts at the base of the cliff. A tiny flower garden occupied the front, along with a large clay statue next to the bamboo door. The figure was only three feet tall, but the big eyes and perplexed expression were unmistakable. "Why do you have a statue of Cimil?"

"She is the goddess who protects us. We serve her and only her."

Oh boy. That can't be good.

"Now get inside." Fina opened the bamboo door. "And if I were you, I would not step outside until I come for you. You are now on sacred land, and your male energy is considered a bad omen."

He might take that as an insult if it weren't for the fact that these women were completely nuts. Anyone who worshipped Cimil couldn't be right in the head.

Brutus ducked inside the small one-room structure and turned to face her. "And what do you believe? Am I poison?"

"I believe that nothing good can ever come from a man except his seed—to make more women, of course."

"That's a little sexist, don't you think?"

She shrugged. "If what you say is true, and a plague is upon us, I assure you it is because your sex has displeased Cimil—the almighty goddess."

He tried not to vomit in his mouth. "Cimil is a—" He was about to say *lunatic* but decided it wasn't wise to insult their favorite deity. "She is sister to thirteen other deities, you know. She is not the *only* god."

Fina smiled. "Stupid man. She is the only one who has the ear of the Universe. Cimil holds our fates in her hands."

That was like saying his left ass cheek could decide the weather. "How do you know this?"

"Time for chitchat is over. Someone will return shortly with clothing and hot water for bathing. You are to make yourself presentable to speak to my mother before dinner." She turned to leave. "Oh. And feed my cat. There's monkey jerky in that chest." Fina left, and he heard something hit the door. Likely a brace of some sort.

Brutus looked down at the little kitten in his arms. "Is she always this grumpy?"

Meow.

"I agree." Fina was wound tighter than a hemorrhoidal vampire. "What do you think will happen to me tonight?"

The kitten looked up at him with its big green eyes. It didn't know.

"Not to worry, friend. I have lived more lifetimes than most men. If they kill me, then I have no complaints." Not exactly true. He had never known the love of a good woman. He'd never had a real family. No one had ever celebrated his birthday, not even him. He didn't know when, where, or to whom he was born. And no one had ever known the real him, the badass man beneath the camo pants.

"Perhaps it is time, my friend, for old soldiers to give up such dreams and step into the eternal abyss." He sighed with a heavy heart.

∂⁂ ⋘

Fina tried to hide her dread with confident strides as she walked away from her hut, where the unfathomably hot warrior man was corralled, but anyone paying attention would know all was not well. The guilt of this situation made her sick. And, well, slightly frustrated, too.

Brutus was the first male she'd ever laid eyes on who exhibited such fierce, virile, sexy traits. Honestly, he made her feel like warm squirrel lard melting over a hot yucca patty. *Sigh...so delicious.*

But, alas, sex was not in the cards for her. Not for a very long time, and not until she was leader—i.e., after the death of her mother. Then and only then would she be allowed to have sex to produce a single daughter. The tribe only bore females and did not want multiple heirs competing for future leader. Competition for power was the way of "those vile men."

Hmmph! As if men were the enemy? As if their all-female tribe was superior? Okay, maybe so, but they still needed men. And regular sex would be nice, too.

Another thing: Why was everyone expected to live like selfless drones? They were not ants. They were great warriors, hunters, and builders.

Gods, I really hate all this. Not that she didn't love her tribe, but the rules, the traditions, the way they all had to pretend to worship Cimil left no room for individuality. Yes, they ate. Yes, they had shelter. Yes, the women received a basic education here in the village, but it wasn't even close to the schooling she'd received on the outside. And not everyone pulled their weight. What was the incentive? You worked more or worked less, didn't matter. Everyone got the same thing. A crappy hut with a leaky roof and two meals a day.

Then there was the money situation. They might be isolated from the world, but they didn't believe in remaining ignorant when it came to the outside world, so the tribe had to make some money—enough for one person to get a formal education. Yes, she was that person. She had been charged with passing her knowledge to the entire tribe so they might stay up to speed on modern life, mostly for the purpose of creating contingencies against intruders. For this reason, they sold exotic flowers to a few perfume companies, but that only left them with enough funds to send one person to a real school.

But why only one? Maybe others might like a formal education, too.

Theoretically, they could take the money for that single, outrageously expensive Ivy League degree and send ten highly motivated members to a good school. If more than ten wanted to go, then allow the best, most intelligent to compete. Honestly, it was better than today's system, where they spent all their cash on just one individual, while the rest of the tribe received barely anything. Old books, an older teacher (nearly six hundred years old), and one abacus. *Seriously?*

That led Fina to her next thought: Her mother refused to consider changing anything, including modernizing their business so that they might responsibly grow and harvest more flowers. Those were unearned profits they could use to better the lives of everyone, including sending more tribes-women to a formal school if they chose.

Her mother called Fina's ideas "greedy." She said that money would corrupt them all.

But was that so? Growing more flowers wouldn't make them millionaires, but it would certainly fix the leaky-hut situation. And it wasn't as if anyone would be forced to work longer hours. Those who wanted dry beds could put in the effort and longer hours in the flower field. Those who didn't want to work longer and liked being rained on could continue doing what they were doing. The minimum.

There was no judgment here. To each her own.

But what killed Fina was that her mother wouldn't even entertain giving their people a choice. "My job is to care for them, provide for them," she'd say. What her mother really meant was that *they* did all the work and *she* got all the power. Mother treated them like children and decided what they ate, what they wore, how many hours they worked, and what duties they performed. Dreaming was *not* allowed. Having diversity in thought was *not* allowed. Self-determination was *not* allowed.

Because failure was *not* allowed.

I just don't get it. Why send me to school and fill my head with so many ideas, only to tell me I am not allowed to use them? The last time she went against her mother with one of her "radical" ideas, she had been accused of heresy. *I just said I didn't think we all had to worship Cimil. Maybe we could choose whom we adored.*

Speaking her mind had cost Fina three weeks tied to a black palm. And those fuckers hurt. The porcupine of plants.

When Fina became queen, she would allow everyone to have their own ideas, to worship the deity of their choosing. She would let men in the village, and she'd have sex every day, as much as she liked, and she might not even have children. Or she might. Either way, it would be her choice, and if there was no heir, then they'd let the members compete for the spot. Hell, maybe she'd let them do that anyway. Puzzles, hunting, swimming, and running. Why not? Their tribe claimed to value intelligence, bravery, and resilience. Let those be the job interview.

As for the lost art of thinking, Fina would make it mandatory for people to use their gods-given brains to discuss topics, even if they disagreed. Just as her professor had taught her in debate club at the university. You were assigned a topic and had to make an argument regardless of your own position. As a future leader, she found this exercise extremely valuable. It taught her to really see the world from another person's point of view, something of great value when trying to build bridges and loyalty instead of ruling by fear.

But, alas, as things stood today, Fina would be hung from the highest cliff for daring to say a word if it didn't fall in line with her mother's thoughts. *Treason! Die! You are worthless. How dare you contradict me.*

Ugh. How could her mother claim to have a good heart, to value respect, and love her fellow woman? This was not love. It was guilt, fear, and control packaged as loyalty.

Which led Fina to her biggest gripe of all: Men. Or, really, impregnation and men. *Also, mannibalism. Yuck.*

The lore said that the women of the tribe could only be impregnated after their centennial birthday. On a full moon. When the kapok tree near the bend in river had its first blossom and the wind blew due north.

So for pregnancy to happen, they'd have to allow many, *many* men into the village at the right time of year so they'd be present at the precise moment.

But men were banned altogether now because that crazy redheaded goddess had showed up one day, many centuries ago, and spouted off about toxic masculinity. "Allowing men into the village will make you weak."

No one questioned Cimil. No one looked at the facts. They simply took Cimil's word. Why? Because she was a goddess? There was no proof that men made women stupid.

Okay, maybe there was proof, like in the case of someone like Brutus, who sucked the thoughts from her mind, but that was a different animal. Men in general did not hold such power over the opposite gender.

Nevertheless, a tragedy was in the making. No men meant no babies. No babies meant the end was inevitable. There'd be no new warriors to take over when death finally caught up with them all. Immortal or not, no one truly lived forever.

Our own blind faith in Cimil will be our downfall.

Which led Fina to her final thoughts about tonight: Was Brutus truly the nail in their coffin, as Cimil had prophesied? *"A male of unspeakable strength, beauty, and kindness will invade your lands and mark the beginning of the end."*

In her mind, the word of Cimil carried about as much weight as a gnat's ass. Brutus was not here to bring about their destruction. And according to him, Cimil had actually sent him! To save them! He certainly was no destroyer of "their way." Brutus exhibited signs of loyalty, sound-mindedness, and patience. The nonstop mounting was proof. Any other male would have taken his own life by now. But, Brutus, he hung in there. *Or…stood in there?*

Anyway, he did whatever erect and very determined penises on a mission did.

I hope everyone listens to him tonight. If she was right, then he'd truly come with a message meant to foster their salvation.

Sadly, however, despite his motives, Fina knew her tribe would not forgo the cleansing ritual: Any male who stepped foot on their sacred female land had to be devoured in order to ensure their toxic man-juju was abated. She was among the youngest of the tribe, so they'd probably offer her the balls. She didn't care how sacred this ritual was, she could never snack on a man's undercarriage.

Mannibalism is gross.

But, alas, as future leader, she had to choose her battles. The survival of her tribe might very well rest on Brutus's message. It was far more important that they listen to what he had to say. If he became stew afterward, it would be most regrettable, but not her biggest problem.

Fina shivered, visualizing Mittens, the village pet, picking Brutus's bones clean. *I am sorry, sweet kitten-rescuer, but I cannot save you.*

CHAPTER SIX

Zac, God of Pure Fucking Pissed-Offness, cussed at the dripping ceiling of the sparkly cave. If he never met another unicorn for the duration of his existence, it would be too soon. Minky was a furry little bitch to leave him like this.

Alive, no less! She hadn't even had the decency to murder him.

Now how will I get a new body? He needed to find Tula—or at least her spirit—and tell her he was okay and that, come underworld or high water, he would reunite her soul with her petite little body, which came equipped with every bump, bell, and whistle a guy like him appreciated, including big innocent blue eyes, a perky nose, and pouty lips. Tula was the first woman ever to light him up like a supernova on Earth's birthday. Fireworks. That was what he saw when they kissed, when he touched her and held her. Not that they'd been intimate before, but he'd imagined it a thousand times.

Of course, if for some reason she couldn't be reunited with her body, he'd take her just as she was. *Hell, I wouldn't be the first deity to fall for a ghost whose body is locked away inside an evil horny magical beast.* All he wanted was to be with her.

Wait. Maybe that's the loophole! He'd never told Minky he'd be faithful. He'd only said he'd pay whatever price to free Cimil—the only one who supposedly knew how to reunite Tula with her preserved body. Minky had then said, "The price is you. I want you." But Zac had never told Minky he'd be exclusive or even have sex with her, so if that meant the three of them had to become a trio, so be it. Minky would learn what it felt like to be unloved, rejected, and hated even. Perhaps she would move on. If it took a millennium, he didn't care.

"Oh, Tula," he sighed, "I can put up with anything except an existence without you."

"Zac? Zac! Are you here?" called out a small female voice.

"Tula?" Could it be her?

"Yes! Zac! Ohmygod!"

Before he could blink, Tula's small form appeared before him, her pale cheeks stained with tears.

"I thought I'd never find you." She covered her mouth and began hiccupping.

He hated to see his mate cry. "Ssssh now. I am here, my love."

"I-I-I have been to every despicable place I could think of where a unicorn might hide a sex slave: brothel, kink bar, M&M club."

"You mean S&M?"

"No. I mean a place where unicorns go to swap

the M&M colors they don't like. It's a thing."

It was? "How did you find me here?"

"I once read an article on the internet about the sparkliest places on the planet. This exact cave came up as number two hundred and three on the list. It was referenced in some ancient hieroglyphics on Narmer's temple."

Narmer was an Egyptian pharaoh turned vampire. Today, better known as *Roberto,* Cimil's husband. Minky, Roberto, and Cimil had a long history.

Wow. Did Tula have a memory or what? But Zac always said she was smart. *She fell in love with me, didn't she?*

"You are indeed the smartest woman I have ever met, Tula." He glowed with pride.

She lunged forward to kiss him but fell through his body into the boulder, where he was bound with supernaturally sturdy chains.

He winced, hearing her whimper. "Are you all right?"

Tula's tiny head popped out of his chest.

He yelped. "Gods, woman! Don't do that."

"Sorry!" Tula righted herself and stood in front of him again in her orange muumuu. Very sexy. He liked a conservative woman who hid everything—made it so much more fun to tempt them. "Didn't mean to scare you."

"I am a god. Nothing scares me. Except unicorns."

"Ditto."

"Speaking of," he said, "we must hurry before Minky returns. I need you to end this body."

Tula stared up at him in wonder. "But why?"

"I will be sent back to my world, get a new one. From there, I will go to my brethren and tell them what Minky has done. We will force Cimil to step in and make her stupid pet give you your body back."

Tula's tiny little mouth twisted.

"What? It is an excellent plan. Also, if Cimil refuses, I've already decided that Minky cannot stop us from being together. Let her watch our love from the sidelines. I call it my Third Wheel plan."

"It's just that while you've been away, things have gotten worse." Tula went on to explain that the plague situation was spiraling out of control, spreading to just about every single immortal on the planet. "Zac, as much as I love you and want my body back, your brethren need you right now. Humanity needs you."

Dammit. She was right. Was an awesome god's work ever done?

"Very well." He sighed. "I will do my duty, but after that, my attention will go to you and only you." There had to be a way to get Minky to cough up that body. "Now, if you don't mind, could you collapse the ceiling? I need to die and get out of here."

"But I can't move anything solid."

"That is why we are in luck; this cave is one giant unicorn toilet. Very magical."

"Sorry?" Tula blinked her wide blue eyes with confusion.

"This is Minky's bathroom. All those sparkly rocks are made of her crap." His eyes swept the cave, which was filled with huge colorful crystals that coated every inch of the place.

"Ewww! Really?"

"Yes. Really." He'd personally watched Minky crap a few times. What killed him was that humans loved to eat this shit. And unicorn snot, boogers, loogies, dingleberries. He'd seen it all for sale on Amazon. They had some strange obsession. He'd even seen canned unicorn farts. *So nasty.*

"Wow. Minky must be really bonkers if she wanted to keep you here."

He shrugged. "I've been in worse places. Like Cimil's basement."

Tula's face contorted.

Ah. See. Tula knew. Cimil had actually hired Tula to work at Immortal Matchmakers, Inc., a dating agency he had been forced to open with Cimil after being banished to the human world. Personally, he never felt like his offense of falling in love with his brother's woman, and maybe trying to steal her way, was anything close to the things Cimil had done—a list too long to mention—however, had he not been banished to play matchmaker, he would not have met Tula, his true mate. Tula had captivated him from day one, and from that point on, it became his quest to be a worthy god she could love. *Winning!*

"So you think I can get the ceiling to crack?" Tula stared up at the enormous dome laden with large multicolored crystals of crap.

"It is worth a try."

"Wow. How does she get her poop all the way up there? And why's it so many colors?" She shook her head. "Never mind. I don't really want to know."

"Good choice."

"If I get the ceiling to collapse, where will I find you?"

It would take Zac three or four days to get a new body and travel through the cenote—an underground spring found deep in the Yucatan jungle, used by the gods as a portal between this world and theirs. Once back in the human realm, he'd have to hike to the nearest Uchben base and catch a plane ride to Sedona, where the gods were undoubtedly coordinating efforts to deal with this plague of evil immortals.

I wonder how their matchmaking efforts are coming along. After all, love was the only cure to what ailed the immortal community.

He was almost tempted to go home, straight to LA first. His laptop was there in the office along with all of the client files. He might have better luck matching people if he had everything he needed.

I wish it weren't such a slow process sorting through all of the profiles and trying to pair them up with someone who shares similar interests. Then there was the lack of females in general. Of course, nowadays, many immortals were hooking up with humans. Like with him and Tula.

Wait! I have an idea. I know how to get everyone mated up. Why had he never thought of this before? The solution to this entire mess, the overnight cure, had been staring him in the face the entire time.

He looked down at his beloved mate. "Head straight to Immortal Matchmakers, Inc., and start going through the files. Make sure everyone is loaded into the system. Oh, wait. Never mind. You can't actually lift and open the files. Just meet me there in the office."

"Why?" she asked.

"Because Zac is officially now the God of Matchmaking, and he's open for business."

CHAPTER SEVEN

Brutus watched the team of "official bathers" exit Fina's hut. No doubt about it, this tribe had some very peculiar rituals. But why they had to shave off his body hair in order for him to speak to the leader tonight, he'd never understand. They'd even shaved his balls. He'd never felt so weirded out. Or had such soft skin. The only thing they left was his facial hair, now a short black beard, and the hair atop his head—a closely cropped crew cut. Then they'd proceeded to bathe him with an odd soap that smelled of sage and rosemary. Finally, they'd oiled him down with sea salt and coconut butter.

"What? Are you going to let me talk to your leader or serve me to her as supper?" he'd asked.

The ladies had burst out laughing.

I guess they think their little customs are a bit extreme, too.

Now wearing a skirt made of banana leaves strung together on a piece of twine, he was ready for his grand shiny, oily entrance.

Through the spaces of the bamboo door in Fina's hut, he noted a bonfire blazing down on the beach, and the night air was filled with *hurrahs* and *cheers.*

I guess these women know how to party. Brutus heard footsteps approaching and glanced down at the little kitten, who was meowing like crazy. "Well, wish me luck, little guy."

The door opened and Zeus bolted.

"Hey!" Fina yelled. "Get back here!"

But the tiny cat disappeared into the shadows.

"Do not fret," said Brutus. "I will help you look for him after I see your mother. And don't you look nice."

Fina wore her long dark hair up in a messy bun and had on a black suede bikini. "Um. Thank you," she said with a stiffness in her tone.

Was she nervous about the outcome of this evening?

"Do not fret, Fina. I am a man of few words, but I can make your mother hear me. Your people's survival depends on it, and I have yet to ever fail a mission."

Fina's dark eyes turned glossy.

Oh, look. She's overwhelmed by my chivalry and dedication to her people's well-being. He reached out and grabbed her shoulder. "No need to thank me. Saving others is what I do."

Fina frowned, the corners of her mouth pulling down. "No, you idiot. It's not that."

"No need for name-calling. Tell me what worries you. I'm sure I can fix it."

She shook her head. "It's just that…that…well,

you're a very beautiful man and…"

Was the little warrior woman blushing? How sweet. "And?"

She straightened her spine and gave her head a vigorous shake. "Never mind. It's all going to be fine." She turned and started walking away, her curvy ass wiggling with a delightful rhythm.

Could stare at that all day. He especially loved her wide hips in that tiny suede bikini.

"Come on," she yelled. "Don't want to keep them waiting."

A peculiar woman, this Fina. Mean to the core one moment and positively weepy the next. *Must be that time of the month. Thank the gods I do not have to deal with such things with my men.* Their equivalent to a period was when they went more than four weeks without getting laid. *So irritable and snacky.*

He followed Fina out of the small garden and down the sandy trail to the beach, where approximately a hundred golden-haired females stood in various forms of dress. Some wore only little skirts made of hides, and some wore suede outfits like Fina's. Honestly, if he weren't so irritated by how they'd all used him for such vigorous sex, he would say they were some of the loveliest females on the planet.

Fina, the only dark-haired beauty among them, stopped beside the enormous bonfire and pointed to the ground. "Kneel," she commanded him.

He came up in front of her and frowned.

Though he considered her to be "little" due to the fact he was twice her size when it came to muscles and torso girth, he was actually only a few inches taller. These women could easily form their own basketball team.

"No," he said sternly, "I will not kneel."

The women gathered around and snickered.

Fina's tanned face turned an angry red. "I said *kneel.*"

Brutus grunted. He could tell he was embarrassing Fina by defying her authority. And, honestly, all he really wanted was to say what he came to say and then get the hell out of there. *I miss my dog.* Though, he might stay for supper. Whatever was cooking in that giant pot off to the side of the bonfire smelled delicious. He inhaled the scent of stewing onions and herbs wafting in the air.

With another grunt, he got to his knees and stared up at Fina. "Fine. I'm kneeling. Can we get this over with now? I have places to be, and this skirt is annoying." The leaf in the back kept sticking in his butt crack. And with a such a large strong muscular ass, he had to tug pretty hard to unwedge it. Very undignified.

Fina was about to speak when the crowd of women parted like the sea.

"All hail Queen Chacacacakhan!" someone called out, and the women bowed their heads.

A tall, statuesque female with flowing waves of raven black hair reaching down to her waist appeared in a colorful wooden mask.

Did they just call her...Chaca-caca-khan? He tried not to laugh. What a silly name. *I wonder what it means. The caca queen perhaps?* Or maybe she was a fan of Cha-Ka, from that wonderful TV show *Land of the Lost*? Or Khan from *Star Trek*? Or perhaps the singer Chaka Khan.

I'm going with door number four. Without argument, the '80s was the most meaningful era of energetic synthesizer tunes meant to evoke the playful spirit within. That's right, he was a fan, and Chaka Khan was an icon of the era, worthy of all ten Grammys under her belt.

And wait. Hold the bonfire... Is that a unicorn mask on the queen's face? Yes, it was. It had a little seashell horn sticking up at the top, covered in glittering gems.

Oh, gods. These women really did have a thing for Cimil. Not a good sign. He could only hope they weren't as irrational and devious as the Goddess of the Underworld.

"Introduce yourself!" demanded the queen, who wore a rainbow-colored toga that dragged in the sand. In her hand, she carried the biggest fucking battle-ax he'd ever seen, the handle wrapped in ribbons of pinks, reds, and yellows.

So they're warriors with flair. He could respect that. He himself liked to hang his lucky Maaskab ear from the hilt of his sword. That evil Mayan priest had been his first official kill centuries ago.

Had it encased in silver.

"Good evening," Brutus said. "Thank you for agreeing to see me." Finally. "I am—"

"Silence!" The queen stepped forward, reached down, and slapped him. "You do not speak unless spoken to, man."

"Ow." He covered his cheek. "Didn't you just say to introduce myself? And is hitting really necessary?" Not even he hit a foe without just cause. It was the code of warriors. Never harm those who don't stand in your way or pose a threat. Everyone else? Ass kicking.

The women gasped at his perceived insolence.

The leader raised her hand once again, but this time, he wasn't having it. Leafy skirt or not, he could still kick all these girls' asses.

I hope? They did look pretty tough.

He got to his feet and rose to his full height, staring down at the woman. "I haven't come this far to be slapped. And might I remind you that if it weren't for men like me, specifically me, you wouldn't be here right now. I am an esteemed Uchben leader who has halted more apocalypses than you have years on this planet, which means I am to be respected."

"You will kneel, or I will remove your head." The leader lowered her battle-ax and pointed it at him.

"Mother!" Fina stepped forward. "He comes with a message from Cimil. She asked him to be here."

Though he couldn't see the queen's face, he suspected her mouth was hanging open. "Cimil sent him? A man? Here?"

"Yes! That's what I was trying to tell you earlier."

Everyone gasped. What was the big deal?

"Actually," Brutus cleared his throat, "I come on behalf of all the gods. With a warning and an invitation." He went on to explain about the plague and how the queen's people would be afflicted. "Any day now, it will reach you, and when it does, you will turn evil. You will fight each other, you will want to kill for fun, and you will destroy anything that gets in your way."

"Um. Kind of like we already do?" piped up one woman.

The rest laughed. Did they think this was a joke?

"You do not understand," Brutus tried to explain. "If you flip from the plague, the gods will have no choice but to come and imprison you for the good of humans. Anyone who resists will be killed. So, therefore, it is in your best interest to come with me now so that we might assist you all in finding mates." He left out the part that they might be doing it from the gods' prison.

There was stiff silence in the air, filled only with the crackle and pop of the bonfire.

No one moved a muscle or said a word.

Then…laughter. Not just laughter, but hysterical screaming mixed with choking and hacking. Even Fina's mother joined in.

"Everyone!" Fina cried out. "Stop that! You need to take this seriously. We will all die by each other's hands if we do not go with him."

But no one listened. Not a soul.

Finally, the queen waved her battle-ax, and the group went silent. She turned her back on Brutus to address the group. "Well, it appears the prophecy is upon us. Just as Cimil foresaw. Word for word." The queen inhaled slowly, the women hanging on her every word. "But we are not cowards! We are warriors! And like the brave fighters we are, we will confront death head-on!"

The women cheered, hooting and howling out their war cry.

Wait. What? "Are you saying you wish to die?" Brutus spoke loudly, trying to address the queen over the noise. "You wish to kill each other, or be hunted and executed by the gods?"

The queen turned to him. "It is our destiny," she said. "It is not our place to question it."

He glanced at Fina standing beside her mother. He could see the torment and anger in her dark eyes. She did not agree, so why didn't she speak up?

"Well, then," he said, "I am very sorry to hear that. Because we could all use your help, including the very brave and loyal soldiers under my command, who, by the way, also deserve your loyalty and respect. More than once, they have put their lives on the line to save every breathing soul in existence. But, right now, they are locked up in a prison because love has yet to find them, and they did not wish to die for something that will eventually get resolved. They want to live and fight another day."

He hoped the leader would catch his meaning. Even his bravest saw the logic in being locked up if they could not be mated.

"Then they are fools," the queen scowled. "Because the great goddess foretold the end, and you cannot escape destiny. You can only die with honor."

He crinkled his nose. "But you do understand that Cimil foresees 'the end' ten times a day, right? Hell, she's usually the one causing it. You can't believe a word from that woman's mouth."

The collective snarls made him realize that he'd crossed the line.

"I'm very sorry," he said quickly, holding up his palms. "I meant no disrespect. But if you would come with me and speak with the other gods, you'd know I'm telling the truth."

The leader said nothing.

"Mother, please?" Fina begged. "At least *you* go with him. I can stay here and—"

"You will be quiet, child," snapped the queen, "or his head will not be the only one stewing in the pot tonight."

Brutus growled. "You do not need to threaten her like—hold on. Pot?" He glanced over at a group of hungry-looking women brandishing very long swords. *How did I not see this coming?*

"Brutus, run!" Fina barked. "Run!" She pushed her mother, who fell back, barely missing the bonfire.

He had never once run from a fight. In fact, it felt so unnatural that it took two full seconds to get his feet moving.

Brutus turned and started sprinting in the opposite direction of the village, toward the thick, dark jungle downstream from the waterfall.

I hope they don't have built-in night vision. Because he sure didn't. "*Ooph!*" He ran into a tree and fell back. Luckily, his body was fairly resilient.

He got to his feet again and continued running. Someone was on his tail. Someone moving faster than him.

But of course. These women had to know the terrain like the backs of their hands. This was their home.

"Run! Faster, you big muscle log!" Fina's voice called out.

She was following him? "What are you doing?" Her mother would not be happy.

"Move!" Fina yelled.

"I can't see where I'm going."

He felt a rough little hand grab his, triggering a wave of odd tingles, and start tugging him along. He didn't know if she'd simply mastered the landscape or truly could see in the dark. Either way, they were moving faster now with her in the lead. Unfortunately, he doubted that would be an advantage. If Fina knew how to run in the jungle, so did the other women.

"Where are we going?" he asked, running behind her as she pushed through wall after wall of vines and branches.

"Off the deep end."

"Very funny. But I assure you your mental faculties are just fine."

"No. I mean we're jumping off the next waterfall downstream into the deep end of the next pool. They won't follow us off sacred land."

"When you say jump off a cliff," he yelled out as they ran, "exactly how high are we talking?"

"Never measured! I'm afraid of heights, remember?"

Panting, he asked, "Then how are you certain it is safe? Because while I am technically immortal, that does require my body to remain in one piece." Not that *he* was afraid of heights—he'd jumped from airplanes plenty of times, but that was generally with the aid of a parachute.

"Not certain at all, but if you want to live…" She skidded to a halt.

He ran into her, slamming right into her back. He wasn't going to pretend that it hadn't felt kind of good.

"Watch it! You almost pushed me over," she said.

"Next time, alert me when you wish to stop running." He never had this issue of communication with his men. Actually, it was the opposite. They communicated too much. Nothing was private due to their telepathy.

"How about you and the General put a sock in it," Fina barked.

"I have no socks. You took them from me," he pointed out.

"Stop it. They're coming. We have to jump."

He hated to admit it, but maybe she was braver than him, especially if she was willing to overcome her fear. "Fine. I'm ready."

She grabbed his hand, and suddenly they were falling into the night.

CHAPTER EIGHT

"Keep moving and stop talking!" Colel, Mistress of Bees, swung her machete, carving a narrow path through the Amazonian jungle while the rain relentlessly pelted her and her immortal hive.

Gods, I really wish I hadn't worn my stupid toga. It was made of a fine cream-colored silk, which she thought would keep her cool in this sweltering heat, but the branches and vines had cut it to shreds.

"And stop laughing at me!" she barked. "I know my ass is hanging out!" *Bees! I swear, for insects with such tiny bodies, they could be huge assholes.* Especially Chuck, the hive leader.

Buzzz. Buzzz. Chuck flew in a circle around her head, weaving between huge raindrops. He continued to chastise her for running off like this and defying Votan. Also, her mate, Rys, wouldn't *bee* very happy either, but too bad. Just because she had made her choice and given her heart to him didn't mean she would abandon Brutus. Fact was, he'd been there for her time and time again as she'd traipsed around the globe to check on her flock. And now it was time for her to give back.

I know something's wrong. I can feel it. Brutus

and she were connected, after all—the Universe's idea of a sick little joke, giving her two men, two options, two mates. What she felt with Rys, however, was infinitely stronger. She loved him with all her heart, but she still cared for Brutus. Probably more than she should. Definitely more than Rys was comfortable with.

Maybe if Brutus finds a love of his own, it will sever our connection. She'd be okay with that. He deserved happiness.

Chuck buzzed at her again and then landed right on her nose, trying to stare her down.

"Okay! I got it. You're wet, hungry, and tired, but I'm the one carrying you fools. So if you want to get out of here, I suggest you all get off your immortal bee butts and start canvassing the jungle for Brutus. Go ask the other hives in the area if they've seen him." They had to have come across him.

Chuck gave the orders, and the tiny gang of black-and-yellow soldiers dispersed from her hat into the dense jungle. Actually, technically they were in the rainforest—lots of tall trees—but from this vantage point, it was all one, big, wet, green mess!

"Thank you!" she called out, because the sooner she found Brutus, the sooner they could all get back to beesness: saving the world.

Colel continued pushing ahead, chopping her way toward the mountain. It was miles away, but the last time she'd come across the tribe of women where Brutus was heading, she'd found their village somewhere near its base, next to an enormous waterfall. *I hope I find them.* With their help, she'd find Brutus for sure. They knew every crack and crevasse of this jungle. They'd know where to look for him.

∾ ∾

Brutus woke to the feeling of warm water dribbling on his face. Well, it was that or a monkey pissing on his head. He cracked open one eye and found Fina leaning over him with a chunk of bamboo in her hand.

"What are you doing?" he asked.

"I made a cup with this bamboo. I'm washing that gash on your head."

"Gash?" he mumbled.

"Yeah. You must've hit something on the way down. It knocked you out. Took me all morning to find you downriver."

He didn't recall any of that. "Lucky I didn't drown."

"Your bloated ego must be very buoyant."

"You're one to talk." He'd never met a woman more full of herself.

"It's called confidence—something real leaders have."

"What do you mean by that?" He groaned and sat up in the moist dirt, pressing his hand over the throbbing spot on top of his head. The knot was the size of a golf ball.

"I mean that you claim to be this great soldier, but you don't know jack shit about assessing an adversary." She huffed. "Can't believe I had to save you."

"Wait. Hold on. Are you saying I should have known your mother was going to have me for supper?"

"Uh, yeah. The savory herbal rubdown should have been a clue. But noooo... You were too occupied with your *important* mission and speaking than you were with sizing up the situation around you. Honestly, if it had been me, I would have been out of there way before dinner. I mean, really? You couldn't have busted through a few bamboo tubes and escaped out the side of my hut?"

Huh. Maybe she's right. He had allowed himself to be tenderized. "I guess it never occurred to me that you were cannibals."

"Ewww. We're not." Fina made a sour face and stuck out her pink little tongue. "We're manni-bals—we only eat men, who aren't technically people under our laws. And we only do so when they wander onto our land. It's believed to be the only way to cleanse ourselves of your bad energy."

Whatever. They still ate people. "How many unfortunate bastards have stepped foot on your holy woman-dirt?"

"I don't know." She shrugged. "Not many.

Though, there was this time about twenty years ago when a mining company sent a party to do soil samples." She sighed. "That was a big haul."

He crinkled up his face.

"Stop it. I didn't make the stupid rule. And for the record, I told my mother I ate some bad pygmy marmoset, so I got out of it."

He continued crinkling his nose. It was just too disgusting for words.

"Well," she lifted her chin, "when I'm queen, I plan to stop the practice and welcome men back into our village."

"Good luck with that." From what he saw, a man had to be pretty hard up to want to spend a weekend at the crazy she-farm, in their crazy cliffside she-huts, being treated like disposable sex pets. "Please be sure to leave me off the invite list."

"No need. It's probably all a moot point now, since I'll be banished. The tribe will never change now, and we'll die off. All because you were too stupid to know you were being set up."

"You could have said something," he pointed out.

"And betray my mother? My tribe?"

"Looks like that's where you landed anyway," he said.

"Yes. And thank you for that!" She shook her head at him.

He was about to say that he never asked for her help, but that would be petty. The fact was, she did help him, and now she would be ostracized. But what would possess her to turn her back on her tribe for a stranger, one she thought so little of?

"Why did you do it?" he asked.

She shrugged and looked away.

Probably just wanted a break from her mom. Couldn't say he blamed her.

"Whatever the reason, I thank you." Brutus got to his feet and dipped his throbbing head in gratitude. "Can't say I've ever been rescued before. Let alone by a tiny feeble woman," he joked.

A feral snarl erupted from Fina's mouth. "Very funny, asshole." She socked his shoulder.

"What?" He stifled a laugh, enjoying irritating her. "Clearly you are a helpless female, but luckily for you, I am here."

She narrowed her dark eyes. "Well, this feeble creature needs food. Oh, and your dick is hanging out."

He glanced down. All but one leaf had managed to survive the journey. He adjusted his hula skirt to hide his cock. "I'm afraid my clothes were stolen by a pack of crazed, sexually ravenous she-demons. But feel free to give me your top. I'm sure I could fashion a man-thong from it."

"Nice try, soldier. But these beauties are reserved for the future father of the next ruler of the tribe."

"You mean you are a virgin?" he teased.

She blushed in response.

Well, well, well… Once again, he found himself trying not to smile. His little warrior princess was a prude. "How adorable."

"Shut up, fucker. It's called tradition. And unlike the men of your era, I care about who I bed. I care whose sperm makes a baby inside me and who will run my tribe when I am gone. Sex. Is not. A pastime."

He studied her for a moment. She'd taken genuine offense. Honestly, her loyalty to the ways of her people was honorable.

"My apologies, Princess Fina." He dipped his head. "I did not mean to disrespect you or your reproductive journey."

"Ugh." She shook her head, grumbling something about how he could shove his "journey" up his ass. "Let's get moving and find something to eat."

"Sounds good." He could definitely go for a banana or mango or whatever was available.

He turned his head to ask her what fruits were plentiful just in time to see her pull a large dagger from the waistband of her little suede bikini bottom. She threw it at a tree, her hand so fast it was nothing more than a blur. When his eyes caught up, he saw a fat, headless fur ball on the ground.

Oh. Poor thing. He winced. At least the squirrel died quickly. The head was completely removed.

"What? You don't eat meat?" she asked, noting his frown.

He did, but he didn't like his meals with the

horror decapitation sideshow. Also, he was partial to squirrels. They were like tiny tree warriors who flew through the air. "I'm watching my cholesterol."

"Whatever." She grabbed her catch and quickly cleaned it.

He was about to ask if she planned to consume it raw—anything was possible when it came to these women—but before he could open his mouth, she had a stick in her hand. She grabbed a small fallen tree limb, drilled a little hole in it with the tip of her knife, and then inserted the tip of her stick. She started rubbing the stick between her palms. Sixty seconds later, there was smoke and an ember. Sixty seconds after that, she had a little fire going using some dead moss she picked off the tree beside her.

He lifted a brow. *Well, that's impressive.* Especially considering they were in the rainforest and absolutely everything was wet.

Fina threw more moss and some tiny twigs atop the flames.

"Are you certain we are a safe enough distance away?" he asked. "Your people might see the smoke."

"We're about a mile off our lands. They won't follow."

He had no reason to doubt her word, but it struck him as odd that her mother would simply allow her to run off like that. Tradition or not, Fina was her daughter.

"All right. So, then, after you eat your breakfast,

what's the plan?" he asked.

"You tell me. You're the one who showed up asking us to go with you."

He rubbed his scruffy chin. The thing was, he didn't know exactly where they were. "There is an old Uchben base about fifty miles north of your lands, but it's vacated." It was where the helicopter had dropped him off.

"Then how were you planning to get home after you came to deliver your super important message?" She made little air quotes around the words *super important*.

"I planned to call for a pickup with my sat phone, which is currently sitting in the backpack you took from me."

"Oh. I burned that."

"What? Why would you do that?"

She flashed an impatient glance his way and speared her now clean and de-furred snack with a roasting stick. "We just don't like having our location tracked, and those satellite devices emit a powerful signal."

"You could have just taken out the battery." She didn't have to toast it.

"I guess that makes you so much smarter than me, doesn't it?"

"Yes," he agreed.

She shook her head. "Hey. Just because I rescued you doesn't mean I have to let you live—and for the record, I own you now."

"Excuse me?"

She pointed her knife at him. "You. Are. Mine. Now. So best watch your tongue because I can do anything I like to you."

CHAPTER NINE

Fina snickered on the inside, watching the wheels turn in Brutus's head. She was messing with him, of course. Their tribe no longer believed in having relationships with men, so why would there be some rule about claiming him as her property? Under the old rule of law, however, she could own him. And keep him in the village. Unfortunately, Cimil had come along.

Nevertheless, it was still fun to imagine him belonging to her. Hell, maybe someday things would change and she could evoke the old laws again.

Brutus stared blankly and folded his thick arms over his bare muscular chest. She tried not to notice how perfectly proportioned he was, right down to the size of his manhood. He was well over six feet tall, with hard bulging muscles on his arms and chest. Even his thighs were impressive. But what captivated her most was his back. It was the back of a warrior—wide and rippling with powerful muscles from swinging a heavy sword. Yes, she could tell. Men who used such ancient weapons had very distinct muscle definition, especially in the lats—unlike a man who simply went to the gym and ended up bulky.

Brutus was built like a battleship. *So hot.* She especially appreciated a warrior who knew how to defend himself with something other than a gun. She herself had trained with the sacred battle-ax that would someday be hers.

Well, maybe not anymore.

"Did you just say you own me?" He pointed to his smooth tanned chest.

"Yep," she lied. "And don't look so surprised. I saved your life, didn't I?"

"Are you certain that you're not the one who hit your head?" His thick dark brows knitted together.

"Hey, those are the rules of our lands. I didn't make them up." Trying not to laugh, she studied his face closely. His pursed lips formed a heart shape when he was thinking. His square jaw also tensed. She liked that there was a certain intensity about him when he used his mind. Thinking was just as important, if not more, than being a skilled fighter.

"We are no longer on your land," he said, "so I am afraid your laws don't apply."

"Well," she stood, dusting the dirt from her hands, "we were on my land when I saved you, and that means my laws were in effect at the time. So, like it or not, I own you now. And trust me, I'm not any happier about it than you are. I mean, look at you. I've never seen such a puny, weak male." Sooner or later she'd let him off the hook, but for now, she was actually enjoying this. She wanted to torment him.

Why? She didn't know.

Perhaps because saving his life had cost her so much. Perhaps because she was angry with her mother and people for refusing to change their savage ways, and Brutus was the only person around to take out that frustration on.

His beautiful turquoise eyes flickered with irritation. He wasn't going for the whole ownership thing.

"Wow. Never took you as a man who lacked honor."

"If I lacked honor," he puffed out his wide chest, "I would have let your tribe simply perish without a thought. Instead, I marched here on foot so you'd have a fighting chance."

"You came because you wanted women for your men."

"So?" He shrugged. "I can't help it if falling in love is the only vaccine."

It was weird how when he spoke of love, his eyes lit up. She'd never met a man, let alone an immortal warrior, who had a romantic streak.

"So who is the woman I am taking you from?" she asked.

"I belong to no one, you included."

Huh. Interesting. So he *was* single. "Then aren't you worried about 'flipping,' as you call it?"

He rubbed his scruffy jaw, producing a bristly sound. "I am technically not singl—you know what?

It is none of your business."

"Okay. Sorry." She held up her palms. "I forgot how touchy your gender can be. So fragile," she whispered.

Brutus replied with a grunt. "I'm going to find some new leaves for my skirt while you devour that poor innocent creature. And I suggest you hurry. We have a lot of ground to cover."

"Where are we going exactly?" He hadn't consulted her with a plan.

"The Uchben have a decommissioned base about fifty miles from here. They might have some old equipment in one of the underground storage lockers. I'm hoping there's a radio."

She supposed that plan would have to do. The alternative was hiking to one of the logger roads about eighty miles in the other direction. However, they'd have to go all the way around the tribe's land to get there, which would probably add another two or three days to the journey.

The question was, however, once she returned with Brutus to his world, what next? The only option was to try to get an audience with Cimil and have her talk some sense into the great and all-powerful Queen Chacacacakhan.

Ugh. I so hate that name. It was from their ancient tongue and meant She Who Swings Fastest From the Tall Tree of Wisdom and Crushes Skulls for Fun.

Yeah, their old language was very efficient.

Could say a lot with a few syllables. Her own name, for example, meant the Cold One Who Tears Out Hearts with Her Pinkies and Bakes Them into Holiday Treats. *That's so not true. I don't even know how to bake.*

Fina was about to give her approval for their plan when something rustled in the damp underbrush. She reached for her dagger and held out her hand to Brutus, urging him to be silent. She would protect him.

Meow! Meow!

"Ohmygod! Zeus? Kitty?" Fina couldn't believe her eyes, but there he was. A tiny gold, white, and brown striped face in the bushes. "Oh, you followed us!" She went over to grab the little thing, but it took one look at her and darted straight to Brutus.

She watched as he scooped Zeus up in his large hand. "Well, hello there, little guy. Miss me?"

She snarled at Brutus.

He noticed, offering her a smug grin. "Well, well, well, guess I own *him* now." He turned for the dense foliage. "Come on, buddy. Let's go find you some grubs."

The cat meowed at him.

Dammit. That's my furbaby!

Brutus added, "And we are definitely picking out a proper name for you. Zeus is a loser. Didn't even make the cut as a real deity."

They were gone, and Fina's meat was on fire.

"Crap!" She blew out the flaming squirrelkabob, but her ego was still ablaze. Her mother was a coldhearted dragon lady. The other women were savages. That little kitten was all she had to keep her from losing her mind some days.

Suddenly, Fina heard something else rustling in the brush again, and whatever it was, it sounded big. Perhaps a predator had been tracking Zeus or… It couldn't be one of her sisters, could it?

No. They would never follow a disgraced tribeswoman. Once a person disobeyed the queen, broke the rules, and left the tribe, they were dead to them, not worth spitting on.

Just in case, Fina grabbed her dagger and prepared for hand-to-hand combat.

A statuesque blonde with turquoise eyes appeared. She was naked and beautiful, with smooth, tanned skin and a sheen to her locks that radiated sunlight. Her tits were like two perfect grapefruits, and her little patch of lady-carpet was all neat.

Is it cut in the shape of a butterfly? Fina tilted her head to one side. Whatever the shape, it had little wings.

"Oh. Good morning there. I am Colel." The woman held out a giant beehive as if it were proof of something important. Then she placed it on her head. "I wonder if you might point me towards a tribe of women that lives around here. Kind of aggressive. Tall. Mostly blonde? I'm looking for one of my warriors, who's gone missing. Last we knew, he was heading to see them."

A giant swarm of bees filled the air above the woman, creating a tiny tornado before disappearing into a hole in the woman's hive-shaped hat.

Fina had seen many strange things in her life, and she'd unseen some, too—for example, their invisible magic spirit animal, Mittens—however, she'd never seen anything quite like this.

"Goddess! What are you doing here?" Brutus appeared, hugging Zeus to his chest.

Goddess? She was a goddess? She was *that* Colel?

Fina's eyes washed over the woman's perfect form. Of course she was a deity; her beauty was surreal. It was also the likely cause for Brutus's now sparkling eyes.

It was the same look he'd had moments ago when she'd asked him if he had a woman.

Fina's gaze bounced anxiously between the two as they locked eyes and the air grew dense with emotion. *Ohmygod. He's in love with her.*

A searing blaze of jealousy scorched its way through Fina's body. Maybe because she knew she could never compete with such a divine creature. And maybe, just maybe, she kind of did wish Brutus belonged to her.

CHAPTER TEN

Fina held on tightly to Zeus while their party of three marched through dark, dangerous, and unfamiliar territory toward the Uchben base Brutus had mentioned earlier. It was some fifty miles from her village—a solid three-day journey at a steady pace. But now, instead of hoping to find a radio once they got there, they had a helicopter waiting. According to Colel, she had flown it all on her own to track down Brutus.

Of course she did! Fina thought bitterly. *She's a goddess. She's perrrfect. She can fly helicopters and probably airplanes, too.*

Fina swung her cat-free arm back and forth, clearing a path with the machete Colel had brought along. They were taking turns to make better time. Seriously, though? If those tiny black-and-yellow assassins didn't stop teasing her, she would lose her shit. The big one, Chuck, kept trying to fly in her mouth, ear, and nostril. Colel claimed it was just playfulness, but the little creature kept making goo-goo-horny eyes at her. *Nasty little bee.*

Of course, what should she expect? *Men! Wings or not, they're all the same.* Like children in big bodies. In Brutus's case, his body was a tank, but he was no different. Dangle a pair of perfect boobies in his face, and he got all tongue-tied and doe-eyed.

The way he looks at that goddess, you'd think she farted golden eggs or something. Fina gave the thought pause. *Hmmm…maybe she does.* Fina knew enough about the fourteen gods to safely say they possessed very unusual powers. Akna, for example, was the Goddess of Fertility, and it was rumored that one could become pregnant by simply being in the same room with her. Then there was Ah-Ciliz, the God of Solar Eclipses. Legend said he could block the sun with a twitch of his nose. People said he once caught a cold and sneezed. Afterward, there was no sun for five years and the dinosaurs died. Of course, some also blamed Cimil for that, so who really knew? Point was, these beings were spectacularly powerful. And gorgeous. There was a reason her tribe dedicated their entire existence to worshipping one of them.

"Fina, did you hear us?" Brutus called out.

She flashed a glance over her shoulder at Mr. and Mrs. Perfect Bodies behind her. "Sorry?"

"I think it's time to set up camp and find dinner. We've been at it all day, and a storm is approaching."

Fina stopped and looked up at the dark clouds accumulating overhead. "What time is it?" she asked. That pesky fat little bee bounced on her nose. "Stop it!"

"Chuck says it is six o'clock. On the nose." Colel chuckled. "That Chuck. Such an adorable comedian."

And you're a pretentious uppity princess! No. Wait. Fina was the real princess. Colel was just a lowly, stupid…*Gorgeous goddess with superpowers. I hate her.*

"You all right?" Brutus came around in front of Fina and grabbed her shoulders. He bowed his head and stared deeply into her eyes as if looking for something. "I think you need water. Your eyes look a little yellow."

Oh, great. Now my eyes are yellow. She hated feeling so imperfect.

Brutus added, "I'll fetch water for you and Señor Gato. Why don't you make a fire to keep the mosquitos away, and then we'll think about finding food."

She blinked. "Who is Señor Gato?"

Brutus chuckled with that deep, sexy, baritone voice and plucked the sweat-covered kitten from her grasp. "My new cat." He turned in the direction of the river, which they needed to follow for another day until they reached the bend.

"Hey! You can't rename him. He's my cat!" she called out.

"Oh, poor Señor Gato. Did the angry lady sweat all over you? Brutus will get you cleaned up. And we'll find you some more of those juicy grubs you like." He and the kitten disappeared into the jungle.

A muted chuckle echoed to her side.

Fina turned her head to find Colel setting her hat down on a big mossy rock.

"What's so funny?" Fina growled.

"Nothing." Colel smiled slyly as if enjoying a bit of humor at Fina's expense.

"Then why do you look like my mother when she's hidden a pit viper under my pillow?" Queen Chacacacakhan enjoyed keeping her people on their feet.

"Your mother put poisonous snakes in your bed?" Colel frowned.

"What doesn't kill you…" Fina shrugged.

"Makes you insane. Trust me, I know. Cimil is my sister."

Everyone knew that. The fourteen gods weren't technically related, since they had no parents, but they considered each other siblings.

"You're close with Cimil, then?" Fina wasn't sure if the gods hung out together or did their own thing.

"No one is really close with Cimil besides Minky her unicorn."

"What about her husband?" Legend had it that Roberto, who was once an Egyptian pharaoh, was a tall drink of hot cocoa with abs for days. He was also a very fine warrior—the fiercest, oldest vampire on the planet. *So cool.* Fina liked the idea of having a man others feared and respected. Personally, she'd been taught to look down on the weaker male sex, which made it difficult to respect men. It was a huge conundrum, actually. Men were worthless and feebleminded, yet...she and the other women needed them. And wanted them. And maybe benefited emotionally from their presence.

The tribe sure seemed to enjoy time with Brutus. In fact, it was her sisters who had acted like feebleminded fools in his presence—fighting and turning on each other. They boasted about him coming two or three times in a session. It was disgusting how they lost their composure. *Animals. Sex-starved animals, the lot of them.* All the while, Brutus had kept his composure and remained the gracious guest.

"That is a very good question, Fina. I suppose Cimil's mate knows her well enough, but may I be honest?" Holding a bundle of branches for the fire, Colel faced her.

"Sure."

"Some of my brethren are mated and practically share one brain, one heart, one soul. While that works for some, it does not work for everyone. Some want the journey of getting to know their mate over time—makes it far more interesting, if you ask me."

"Ah. So how long have you and Brutus been mates?" Fina assumed they had something going on since Colel didn't seem entirely crazy, meaning she was mated, and she'd come all the way here to find him.

"Me and Brutus? Yes, well, our situation is complicated."

So they were a couple! Fina felt her heart plummet toward the earth.

"Ah! See!" Colel shook her finger at Fina. "I *knew* you had a thing for him."

"But I would never...I don't want...I mean...he's yours, and I respect that."

"No. He is not mine. Thus the complication. I actually have two mates, a rarity in the Universe. But I chose the other man to be with because our passion is unlike anything I've ever experienced."

"Wait. So you rejected Brutus?" What sort of idiot woman would toss such a man aside? Beautiful. Strong. Fearless. Also, great with kittens.

"I did." Colel nodded. "But I assure you it was because I never felt anything for him aside from a very deep respect and friendship. Otherwise, I would not have made my choice and taken a vampire as a mate." She crinkled her nose.

"Your man is a vampire?"

"I know. Ewww...right?" Colel shrugged. "But the heart wants what the heart wants, and mine fell in love with him. He's actually a demilord now— part vampire, part demigod, so the vampire thing is really a moot point. He can eat normal food and tolerate the sun. Which is great, because he basically spends his days helping me check on the bees of the world, or he's working on his arrangements. He's a florist and loves flowers as much as I do, so…where ya gonna find a guy like that?"

"I suppose that is a rarity." *Personally, I would spit on such a male.* What sort of man played with flowers? "So," Fina ran a hand through her damp, frizzy hair, "you and Brutus aren't a thing. Totally platonic."

"Yep."

"And Brutus is okay with your choice."

"He has to be." Colel shrugged. "It's a done deal."

Then why had Brutus looked at Colel like she was the last vagina on earth? And if *she* had no feelings for him, then why had Colel come all this way?

Something was going on.

"All right, ladies." Brutus appeared with Zeus, holding a large gray fish and a bunch of ripe bananas. "I found dinner. Even Señor Gato approves. He calls dibs on the head."

Brutus looked at Fina and frowned. "Woman, why is there no fire yet?"

She and Colel exchanged knowing, disapproving glances.

"What? I brought supper, did I not?" Brutus said.

"Yes. Yes, you did. I'll make the fire." Fina got to work with her sticks, trying to assess what was going on inside her chest. A huge mixture of emotions. She hated this man. But why? She wanted this man. But why? And she was jealous of this goddess who'd chosen another man. But why? All she could say was that it made her feel vulnerable and weak—something she'd been trained to loathe.

Brutus was making her doubt everything, including her own strength.

Perhaps my mother was right. Men are poison.

CHAPTER ELEVEN

Brutus knew he shouldn't feel so happy to be with Colel, but seeing her radiant smile and his bee friends again warmed his immortal heart.

He and his men had spent most of last year traveling with the goddess around the world to survey the bee situation. Something was killing them off, and no one knew exactly what. Pesticides? Pollution? The angry vibe humans and immortals carried around these days? Bees were very sensitive creatures, subject to all sorts of subtle changes in the environment. Anyway, the time he'd spent traveling with Colel had given him time for some much-needed reflection. Also, it had given him a chance to learn to knit and make several very smart sweaters for Niccolo, his elderly cocker spaniel. *Peaceful times.*

Being with Colel now, despite his broken heart, still gave him a sense of peace. He merely wished his feelings weren't so strong. She'd made her choice, and he was honor bound never to meddle between the couple, so there was no risk of him falling victim to his emotions, but it sure would be nice to get over her.

He watched as Colel carried on a lengthy conversation with her hive. They could never agree on the best route to travel.

"Here. Your portion." Fina held out a little banana leaf with a slice of steamed fish on top.

"Thank you. And thank you for making that fire. It amazes me how adept you are at it."

She shrugged. "Mother banishes us from the village when we're five and won't let us return until we've mastered the skill. That and whittling a statue of Cimil."

"Your mother sent you out into the jungle alone when you were five?"

"Yeah, but I already knew how to make a fire. I started practicing when I was three. That carving, though—phew!—took me months."

Her mother was an evil tyrant. "Do you think you will miss her?"

"No more than she'll miss me. Zero."

"Well, I find it hard to believe. You are a very fine warrior," he said.

"Thanks. Hey, I made you something." She reached behind her and produced a bundle of leaves.

"Is that a new skirt?" he gushed jokingly.

"Yep. And I made the twine a little stronger this time."

"Very thoughtful. Thank you, Fina." He took it and tied it on over his ratty one.

"I did it for me. I'm tired of seeing your ass hanging out."

Liar. He'd caught her staring at it several times. "I thank you all the same."

"No problem."

"May I ask, when we finally reach Sedona, what do you plan to do?" he asked.

"Honestly? I'm hoping I can convince Cimil to talk to my mom before it's too late and my entire tribe kills each other."

He bobbed his head, thinking that one over. Cimil didn't do anything nice unless she had an ulterior motive, generally related to making another person suffer. "Not to discourage you, Fina, but it might be wiser to have a backup plan, just in case."

She raised a dark brow. "Such as?"

"Well, first, I would suggest trying to find a mate. You'll be little use to anyone if you flip."

"Any suggestions on who might fit the bill?" she asked.

He wouldn't mind bedding her to test out some of those peculiar tingles, but that would not be right. She was a virgin princess and, banished or not, she intended to follow her tribe's tradition of remaining that way until she planned to have a child. He couldn't possibly entertain a casual sexual encounter with such a woman when he knew he would never be that man. His heart still belonged to Colel, and he never wanted to be a father. Well, except to Niccolo. And possibly Señor Gato if Fina decided to part with him.

"I happen to know a few very fine warriors who

might be good matches—hunters, outdoorsmen, into opinionated, stubborn women."

She gasped, and he smiled.

"You're a butt," she said.

"Perhaps, but it is a large strong butt."

She stifled her laugh, but Brutus knew he'd gotten her.

"And what about you?" she asked.

"Me what?"

"Aren't you going to try to find a mate?" she added.

Was the little virgin warrior princess putting out a feeler? His ego ballooned, even if honor would never allow him to consider being with her. "I'm afraid my mating days are over."

"But aren't you worried you'll get infected by this thing?" she asked him.

"Doubtful. Because my heart is—"

"She's right, you know," Colel chimed in, sitting on a pile of leaves by the little campfire. "You really do need to find someone."

He narrowed his eyes at Colel. "No interest. Can you blame me?"

Colel rolled her turquoise eyes. "Brutus, you're a strong, intelligent warrior with a big heart. You don't need me to tell you that your heart will mend and your soul will detach from mine."

"How do you know that?" he asked.

"The Universe gave us a special connection, but you still had free will. You still had to accept it. So you can just as easily unaccept it. When you decide to move on, you will. And you will feel nothing more for me than an esteemed friendship."

He wished he felt as certain as she did. At the moment, he still couldn't accept the fact that the Universe had done this to him. Why attach him to a woman who didn't want him? "I'll believe it when I see it."

Colel shrugged. "Well, I'm beat, and we have a long day of hiking tomorrow." She stretched out on the ground and snapped her fingers. "Blanket!" The swarm of bees exited her hat and covered her entire body.

Fina scrunched her pert little nose.

"It is pretty strange to see the first few times, but you get used to it," he said to Fina.

"Are all of the gods so crazy?" she whispered.

"Yes," he replied.

"I heard that!" Colel barked.

He and Fina exchanged smiles. It was actually nice to see this side of her. More relaxed, in her element, not surrounded by the weight of her role. Suddenly, he caught himself gazing into her dark eyes, and she was staring back.

He quickly looked away. He knew better. "Well, uh, guess I'll turn in, too."

"Sure. Okay. I'll keep watch for a while." Fina unsheathed her dagger and dropped it point down in the dirt for easy reaching.

"No need. Chuck is on point," he said. "No one

will be sneaking up on us—those bees are like a thousand tiny guard dogs."

"Really? Are you sure?" Fina asked. "Because there are dangerous things out here."

"Yes. Very sure." He turned his back to her and stretched out over a bed of leaves he'd set down earlier. Honestly, he hated the act of conversing—he'd never been much of a talker—but with Fina, he rather enjoyed it. Which was why it was best not to let things go any further. "Good night."

"Good night," Fina said.

This is such a good dream… Brutus had never felt so hard, so aroused before. He was lying on his king-size bed at his home, a small casita in Arizona he'd purchased a few decades ago for those rare occasions he had downtime. Next to him in that bed was none other than Fina. Naked. Her eyes wide with lust. Begging him to take her hard as she lay back against the crisp white sheets.

"Are you sure?" he asked.

She flashed a seductive grin and batted her eyelashes. "Yes. I want you. I want you to fuck me and make me a woman."

"That's impossible. You're already more woman than any man knows what to do with." He bowed his head and captured her lips, settling his body between her strong thighs. She felt soft and warm beneath him. He loved how her curves seemed to fit perfectly against his body.

He stared into her eyes for a moment, feeling his chest swell. And then, tingles. Oh, so many tingles. He hadn't even entered her yet, but he felt like he might just come.

"Brutus, don't stop," she muttered in his ear.

"Meow."

"Meow?" Brutus looked at Fina's face. "Did you say 'meow'?"

She nodded. "Meow."

Brutus's eyes suddenly sprang open to the sight of two green eyes staring down at him. He blinked.

"Señor Gato? Why are you on my face?" The kitten meowed again, and he realized something was wrapped around his cock. His hard cock.

"Snake!" He jumped to his feet, thinking there was some sort of jungle creature engaging with his privates, but the moment he moved, he saw Fina lying there with her hand in the spot where his groin had just been.

"Brutus," Fina's dark eyes fluttered open, "what's the matter?"

"What's the matter?" he snarled.

By this time, Colel was sitting up, still covered in her bee blanket, looking like a monster from a horror movie. Didn't bother him nearly as much as being fondled so wonderfully in his sleep.

"You, you, you…" He pointed at Fina, but did not want to embarrass her, given she'd also been asleep. And, yes, he'd liked what she was just doing, but that was beside the point. "You frightened me. That's all. Why are you not sleeping over there in your spot?"

Fina rubbed her eyes. "I don't know. I guess I got a little cold or missed Zeus or something."

"But you can't snuggle up to a warrior while he is asleep. What if I had my sword? Or a gun?"

"Sorry. Jeez. I didn't mean to." She actually looked a little embarrassed.

Meow. Meow.

Brutus gave the kitten a sour look. "And you. Stay off my face when I'm sleeping."

"No. That's his battle cry," Fina said.

Kittens did not have battle cries. "Don't be ridiculous."

A tree branch snapped a few yards away.

Colel's eyes went wide. So did Fina's. Someone *was* near.

"Chuck...attack!" Colel ordered. "You two, run!"

Brutus grabbed Señor Gato and then Fina's hand. Colel was on their tail, but off in the distance yelps and screams erupted. Her bees were putting up a good fight, from the sound of it.

"Ow! Ow!"

"They're stinging us!"

"What are those?!"

"Fina! You bitch! We'll find you! You will pay!"

The three of them kept running. In between the

panting, Brutus could hear Fina's sobs. Why was she crying? Whatever the reason, it would have to wait. They needed to get to safety and put distance between them and those women.

CHAPTER TWELVE

Zac, the smartest motherfucking god on the planet, swiveled in his exec chair and stared out at the twinkling LA lights from the fourteenth floor of the Immortal Matchmakers, Inc., office. "I did it, Tula. I did it."

Tula floated over and sat on his lap—well, hovered, really. "I think you definitely increased the odds. That's for sure."

"Are you kidding me? Every single immortal is going to have a mate by week's end. I just know it."

It had truly been a stroke of genius, uploading the tens of thousands of profiles on to Hot Russian Brides dot com. He was always receiving emails from their matchmakers about how horny and desperate those humans were for love. And most of the ladies were beauties. Any man, immortal or otherwise, would be pleased to have such a bride.

"But, Zac, do you really think these women are willing to mate with a vampire? Or demigod? They aren't the easiest to get along with, and the women don't know anything about the immortal world."

"Did you not read those emails I showed you? They said the women were looking for a commitment and hot sex. Who's more committed to that than a vampire or an incubus?"

Tula didn't look so convinced, but Zac was. He knew this was an angle he'd never tried before, and if these women were as gorgeous and desperate as they seemed, there'd be at least five hundred weddings in no time. Then another five hundred. And another.

Just to be safe, though, he would load the army men's profiles onto Gold Diggers dot com, too. He'd read that most of those ladies were from eastern Europe and wanted marriage immediately "to men of worth." Their immortal soldiers were the worthiest. *And they will appreciate a wife who works hard.* Mining for gold was no easy chore.

"Don't you worry, Tula. All will be set right again in the world by month's end, and with the gods feeling less stressed out, they can set their energy to helping us."

"I hope so, Mr. Zac." Tula popped up from his lap and stared out the window. Several moments later, she began to sob. "I don't like being dead."

"Oh, my love." He got up and pretended to cup her sweet pale cheek. "Don't you worry. I will fix this, and we will be together. Soon. Very soon."

She wiped a tear from her eye and sniffled. "Are you sure?"

"As sure as the day I met you and knew that I would get into those giant panties of yours." Everything would work out because it was destined

so. And because he loved everything about Tula.
Her sweet demeanor, her ultra-unsexy undergar-
ments, her potato-sack-like frocks.

Tula sniffled, but refused to meet his gaze.

"Now, now. Chin up, my dead little buttercup.
Let us depart now for Sedona and break the good
news to my brethren. The end of this plague is
near." With so many immortals soon to be mated,
the Universe would have to give up and move onto
her next hula contest.

"I sure hope you're right, Mr. Zac, because…"

Tula's voice changed ever so slightly. An odd
fluctuation. "What?"

"No. Never mind."

"You must tell me, Tula. I am your mate. There
can be no secrets between us."

She looked away, once again gazing out the
plate-glass window at the cityscape, seeming more
forlorn than ever, which was odd. They were close
to winning this war. He'd just told her so!

"Tula?" he urged, wanting more than anything
to touch her, hold her, fuck her into the next
century.

"I didn't want to tell you, but…" She exhaled.
"I'm fading."

"What?"

"I'm fading," she whispered. "My light is weak-
ening."

He blinked. "What are you talking about?"

Her big blue eyes met his. "My time here with

you is almost up. If I don't get my body back soon, I will have to cross over."

"Says who?" He refused to believe it.

"Just promise me, Mr. Zac, no matter what happens, you won't make any more deals with that unicorn. I'd rather end up in Cimil's basement for all eternity than see you with someone you don't love and who only wants you for your spectacular body."

It was true. It was spectacular. His long black hair and tall ripped body were the embodiment of male perfection. However, he couldn't make such a promise. "Look into my eyes, Tula. I would pledge my soul to Cimil's naked clown army if it meant saving you. Your beautiful life ended too soon, and if it's the last thing I do, you will get to breathe again. Even if it's without me."

He could tell from Tula's expression that she did not agree, but hopefully there was still time to convince her to keep living no matter what.

"Come, Tula. The plane is waiting to take us to Sedona." He turned his head, but Tula was gone.

"Tula? Tula!" She did not reply.

Fuck. He grabbed his laptop and cell and headed out the door. He dialed Cimil's phone, but Roberto answered.

"Get Cimil on the phone," Zac commanded.

"Sorry, she is not here."

"Where is that evil shrew?" he growled.

"Do not talk about my wife like that, and the

evil shrew said she had to run some errands."

"Dammit!" That could mean anything, such as Cimil was out riding Big Foot or time traveling without permission again. *Poor dinosaurs. Why did she have to mess with them?*

"Roberto, if there is even one tiny cell of compassion in that undead heart of yours, I beg you to convince Cimil to make Minky give Tula back her body. Before it's too late."

"I am sorry, brother, but if I've learned one thing about my beloved mate, the moment you ask her to do something, she does the opposite. She cannot help herself. It is the way of chaos, and you know how she loves it so."

"Then...then...tell her to keep us apart! Tell her you hate me and wish to see me suffer without my mate for all eternity!" The signal began to cut out as the elevator doors closed.

"That would be lying—"

The call went dead.

Zac looked at his phone. "You useless fucking pharaoh! I curse you and your children. Who are already cursed."

That had been a waste of time. *Stupid god. Stupid!* Sometimes he wished he'd been born as smart as he was beautiful. He should have known that Tula couldn't remain on this plane of existence forever. Sooner or later, the Universe comes calling and wants its energy back.

If he wanted their story to end happily, he

would have to pull out all the stops. *I simply hope I am not too late.*

෨ ෬

"Dammit! Where the fuck is everyone?" Votan, God of Death and Massive Coronaries, pounded on the stone conference table in the great hall. Not one damned god had dialed in to his mandatory Zoom meeting. Did they not understand they were in the middle of a massive plague and needed to connect as a team in order to triumph?

"Yo. Hey, dude." Votan looked on the giant screen that was supposed to be projecting the faces of his brethren, only to find some wanker wiggling his wanker.

Zoom bomber.

Votan picked up his cell and dialed the chief Uchben, Gabrán. "There's another one." Votan listened and nodded. "Yes. He's showing me his penis." Votan listened. "Yes, that would be lovely. Thank you."

Votan ended the call and then the meeting. *Well, at least I will derive some satisfaction from knowing that in thirty minutes, this bomber will wish he was never born.* Once the Uchben got done with him, he'd never want to see a toilet again. *The flush torture is most effective.*

Votan ran his hands through his long hair. "Gods, what is happening?" And why was no one calling in? This was the fifth day in a row. Granted, everyone was out in the field, helping to round up flipped immortals, but they still needed to set aside two minutes to touch base.

We're never going to win this war. He sank down into his chair and whooshed out a long breath. He didn't care one little bit about himself, but his children deserved better. His wife deserved better. Humans deserved better. But immortals were going mad, burning down buildings, going on killing sprees, shoplifting. In the south, a group of vampires had wiped out entire cities of red wine. A very mean thing to do. The incubi, though there weren't very many left in this plane of existence, had been poking tiny holes in condoms at every drugstore they could find. And just this morning, there were reports that the sex fairies had taken over Twitter and started a negative campaign against the gods. The worst part was, all that negativity was overflowing and catching on in the human world. People were growing more and more agitated by the day. Overnight, the world had turned into a vat of rage.

How did this happen? In his mind, looking back over seventy thousand years, humankind had been on the verge of a major breakthrough. In the last hundred years, incredible progress and change had been made—medicine, access to education, equality in the laws, equality in people's hearts, the quality of life, personal transportation. People were waking up and finally beginning to understand that the only thing that could save them was love, respect, and compassion. But those alone weren't enough. Self-determination, the ability to carve out one's place in the world, was paramount. Being free to make your own destiny was…was…well, it was fucking fantastic!

How did he know this?

Because the gods had been evolving, too, forced to keep up with the flock they were meant to protect. This very recent chapter of enlightenment in humankind's story had sparked a massive revolution among him and his brethren. For the first time ever, they were sharing powers with mortals, opening their hearts to love, and having families. They themselves had begun to see that the gods were not put on this earth to be obeyed and worshipped for their beauty and perfection, though they were beautiful and he was perfect. The gods were here to prevent certain evil humans from destroying the world while they went through their ideological childhood. That was, after all, where humans were in the grand scheme of things. It had taken millions of years to get them out of the caves and to form societies. It would take tens of thousands of years for them to evolve and reach their full potential. *If they survive the transition to adolescence.*

In a matter of weeks, love had been replaced by hate. Fear had replaced hope. People were suddenly focused on the past instead of the future. They were blind to all the good in the world.

But alas, he could do little now, other than stand back and allow destiny to play out. His plan of rounding up the afflicted immortals was failing. Fact was, his small group of mated "soldiers" were no match for the hordes of vampires, demigods, and other creatures provoking mayhem.

We're finished. And the sad part was, the Universe was behind it.

"Votan?" A sweet soft voice spoke behind him. He turned his head to see his red-haired beauty wearing an emerald green dress. His favorite dress. "Emma? What are you doing here? Where are the children?"

She beamed up at him. "With the sitter."

"You left them in New York?" That was their usual home base. Emma grew up there.

"No. They're in your bungalow here in the compound." She toggled her head. "My big strong deity needed us, so here we are." She stared up at him with her dark green eyes. "I could sense your turmoil."

He nodded solemnly. There were no secrets between them, their bond was too strong. He should have known he wasn't going to be able to spare her from this.

"It's bad, isn't it? The plague is getting worse," she asked quietly.

"Worse than bad. I see no way to win." Which was why he wanted to say so many things to her, starting with all of the regrets and pain he'd caused when they first met. Along with most of his brethren, he had been trapped in a cenote by those evil Mayan priests, the Maaskab. Decades went by, and then one day, from the watery depths of his prison, he heard a baby cry. A freakin' baby.

Why? he'd asked. Why was he able to hear this child who was of no use to him or his brethren in terms of being freed? He figured it was just another of the Universe's sick jokes. Until the day he heard the child's first laugh. It was a special magic that luminated his soul. Then he heard her first words, felt her first crush and heartbreak, and experienced everything else in between. And when she became a woman, he began to sense who she truly was. Not a child. Not a weak human. But his mate. Okay, it actually took him a while to accept it because she was so feisty, and he really didn't like her smart mouth. Eventually, though, he fell in love.

Since then, he and Emma had been through so much. Wars, near deaths, breakups, makeups, loss, and the joy of children. Emma always said that she'd never meant to fall for him, that it was an accident, but he knew; they were destined to be together.

"I love you, woman."

Emma's pale cheeks blushed. "Oh, stop it. You know I hate it when you call me that." She grinned.

"But you are, you know. My woman. Now and forever. No matter what."

She frowned with confusion. "Why are you talking like that?"

"Like what?" he asked.

"Like this is the end."

He swallowed down the truth, the cold hard reality that had been rearing its ugly head deep inside his gut. He was talking like this because it very well might be the end, and there was nothing the gods could do.

Perhaps humans and immortal-kind would continue on. Perhaps not. But deep inside he knew that the gods had outlived their usefulness. And, as anyone who knew the Universe would tell you, everything in existence must have a purpose. A place.

The gods were about to be retired. For good. They'd served their purpose.

Which meant the path the world and humans were on was their own. War. Hate. Rage. Destruction. The end. Or they could choose something else. To fight for love. To see the goodness in life and foster every speck of joy they could find. Whatever they chose, it was up to them. The gods had merely been a seventy-thousand-year-old set of training wheels, and those wheels were coming off.

That's what this plague is about. The Universe was forcing the issue. People had to choose. Love or hate. Survival or destruction. And it was up to them. Free will and all that.

"Guy? I don't like that look on your face. You're scaring me," Emma said. Guy was the name she'd given him long ago when she could hear his voice in her head and thought she was going mad. He'd refused to tell her his true name for fear she might research him and find out he was nothing but a poor forgotten god trapped somewhere in the Mayan jungle by a bunch of evil priests. He had not wanted to appear weak in front of her.

Votan hugged her tightly. "No need for worry, my sweet. All will be well."

"You promise?" She pulled away and stared up at him with the same adoration he'd witnessed when they met. Did she have any idea how special she made him feel?

He brushed back her red curls. "I promise. Everything will turn out exactly as it's meant to."

"I love you. You know that, right?"

"I do."

"Good. Because whatever happens, our love is the only thing that matters. Well, that and our spoiled-rotten children. But you get my drift, right?"

He nodded. "Yeah. I get your drift. What do you say we take a quick vacation? You, me, the kids."

"To the villa in Bacalar?" she asked.

"Yes."

"Ohmygod. We haven't been there in forever. Yes! Yes! When can we leave?" she asked.

"Just call the nanny and have her pack the children's swords and clothes. We can go immediately."

"You're sure it's okay?" she asked. "I mean, we are in the middle of another apocalypse."

"There's always an apocalypse. And I see no point in saving the world if I never get to spend time with the only things that truly matter in it."

She stood on her tiptoes and pulled his nearly seven-foot frame down to her, reaching for a kiss. "I fucking love you. You know that, right?"

"And I love you, Emma. Forever."

"Good. Because you're stuck with me until the end."

He nodded solemnly, masking his grief. "Yes, until the end."

CHAPTER THIRTEEN

Brutus was impressed by how resilient and determined Fina was. Dare he say, his little leaf skirt was chafing in a new place, a place where the chubby General kept poking out his head. He wished he could stop and attend to it—yes, yes, in a dirty way—but they'd been running all day with those Amazons on their trail. These trackers showed no signs of giving up.

Well, neither will we!

"How much farther do you think it is?" Fina panted from a few feet back. "We'll need to stop soon and give Zeus some water and food."

"You mean Señor Gato?" Brutus called out, winded from the running.

"Stop it," Fina threw back.

"Chuck sent a scout ahead to measure the distance to the base." Colel spoke loudly, not even a little winded. She was keeping up just fine and continued to deploy her hive to slow down Fina's stalkers. "Hopefully, we'll hear back soon."

"But what if it's too far?" Fina asked. "The trackers are close, no more than ten minutes."

It was a good question. He and Fina would

eventually have to stop and rest. Immortal or not, they still needed fuel to make their bodies go. *And poor tiny kitten must be getting thirsty.* Unfortunately, they'd stopped following the river hours ago, and the next water source would be at the abandoned Uchben base, where they had a well.

"Do you think they know where we are going?" Brutus asked.

"Yes. My people have lived in these jungles for centuries. So if you're thinking we can lose them, forget it."

"What if we split up?" he asked, trying to come up with a way to divert them.

"They are the best trackers in the world and travel in packs of eight. Whichever way we go, even if we split up, they will follow."

He still wondered why Fina's people had come at all. According to Fina, they would not bother. "What do you think they want?" he asked.

"My head. On a stick."

"Because you saved me," he assumed.

"Because my mother can't stand to be disobeyed by her own daughter," she replied.

Suddenly, he heard Fina yelp. When he glanced over his shoulder, she was on the jungle ground, gripping her ankle.

Brutus rushed back to have a look. "What happened?"

"Ow! Ow! Ow!" Fina winced. "I think I broke it."

"How?" he asked.

"I stepped on that rock and lost my balance." She pointed to a stone the size of her fist.

Colel came up on their flank, still naked as a baby save for her living bee bikini. "What happened?"

"She thinks it's broken," Brutus said.

"Oh my," Colel said. "Well, I can carry you."

"No," Fina protested.

"Then I will carry you." Brutus crouched to scoop her up.

"To what end? That will only slow you down, and then not only will the trackers hurt you and Colel, but Señor Gato will get caught in the crossfire."

She'd called him Señor Gato. "What do you propose?" he asked.

"Look, Brutus, I appreciate the fact that you believe you're a powerful warrior," she wiggled her hands toward the sky like two tambourines, "but the truth is, I saved *you*. I got *you* to this point, and I did it because you're weak."

"Weak?" He frowned.

"Yes. Weak. I didn't say anything because what would be the point? Your ego is so bloated that you'd never believe it or listen to me. But hear me now, oh cocky one, I only planned to take you as far as your base and then return to my village to confront my mother and take over in the challenge ritual."

Challenge ritual? "How come you never mentioned this?" he asked.

"Because you wouldn't understand—having a
penis, and all. But now that doesn't matter. You
need to accept that you are but a child I only saved
due to its innocence. Honestly," she sighed, "killing
stupid things is not right."

Stupid things? "You think I'm stupid?"

"I'd spell it out to you, but I doubt you know
how to read. Did you even finish high school?"

"There was no such thing when I was a youth,
but yes, I read very well."

She clapped and offered him a dour look.
"Congrats. Well, maybe when you get home, you
can use that skill to get a clue. By the way, *clue* is
defined as a fact or piece of evidence leading to the
truth." She crinkled her nose. "In this particular
case, the clue is telling you bye-bye."

Brutus stared. He had never encountered such a
cruel-hearted woman, but if she truly thought so
little of him, then why risk life, limb, and paw to
save her? "All right. We will go on without you, but
I'm keeping the cat." He turned and started marching away. "Come, Chuck!"

The bees swarmed around him, leaving Colel
completely bare again. Over time, he'd developed a
strong relationship with the flying perverts and
knew summoning them would persuade Colel to
continue on with him. No argument. A warrior
learns a thing or two when traveling around the

world with a goddess.

"Hey! My bees!" Colel called out.

He ignored her, but felt the need to leave a few parting words for Fina. "And good luck with those bottom-feeding haters you call 'people'!"

"No luck required, Brunhilda! Unlike you, I'm an actual warrior! Born this way—didn't take me centuries to grow half a pair!"

He huffed and stomped ahead, holding the fur ball to his bare chest. "Not to worry, SG. All will be well now that we are rid of that horrible woman." Brutus marched on ahead, barely able to hear a thing since the hive was all around him.

A half hour later, Colel caught up with him and cut him off. "Brutus! Stop!"

"What?" he snapped, feeling rage rolling around in his gut.

"Bees! Hat!" she yelled, and her critters obeyed, going into their hive. "I've been yelling for over a mile." Colel's face was bright red.

"Sorry. Couldn't hear you."

"Yeah. No kidding. Which is very unfortunate."

"Why?" he asked.

Colel gave his shoulder a push. "Because then you might've heard me telling you not to leave. Oh, and to help me fight off Fina's sisters!"

He frowned. What was she talking about? "Weren't you behind me the entire time?"

"No, stupid! Fina's ankle wasn't broken. She was just taking one for the team so we could get away."

Huh? "No—but—she…" He shook his head. "I don't understand."

"I could hear the lies in her words, and if you'd been paying attention, you would've too. Broken ankle? Seriously, Brutus? That girl has a thing for you and just wanted you to go on ahead. She threw herself under the bus. I stayed and tried to reason with Fina, but she wouldn't have it. Then the trackers arrived and took her."

"What?"

"Yes. And look." Colel showed him her arm. "One of them scratched me with something and knocked me right out. A poison or something. I don't think I was out very long though." She smacked her hat. "Thanks a lot, guys! Little bastards," she grumbled.

Meanwhile, Brutus's head began spinning. It simply wasn't possible that he hadn't detected her lies. He was an immortal soldier who'd interrogated hundreds of foes. He could sniff out BS from a mile away. *Yet I fell for it.*

He shook his head. Perhaps Fina was right about one thing; his ego was bloated. And wily, cunning woman that she was, she knew how to use it to achieve her goals.

Brutus took the kitten and shoved it at Colel. "See to it that Señor Gato gets a good drink of water and some food. Please call my men back in Sedona and check in on Niccolo."

"Where are you going?" Colel asked.

"Where do you think?"

"Alone? But, Brutus, you are no match for those women. You *will* die."

"Then I will, but at least I'll die with honor." He started walking away.

"But, Brutus, we are—"

"Good luck with the apocalypse! Kiss your bees for me."

ॐ ॐ

Was he mad? Colel shook her head as Brutus's mighty frame disappeared into the dense, sticky rainforest. Those women were absolutely going to tear him limb from limb, and there wasn't a darn thing she could do about it.

"But, Brutus!" she called out. "We're only five minutes from the old base!"

No reply. He was either out of earshot or ignoring her.

Ugh! Why don't they ever listen? Her plan was to fly north to the new base and gather reinforcements. The women who had Fina were traveling on foot, so Colel could probably cut them off before they reached their village. Once they had Fina back, the soldiers could start rounding up the other ninety or so women, which had to be done anyway before they flipped.

Dammit. "Now what am I going to do?" She

looked down at the sleepy little creature in her arms, nestled against her chest. Brutus was going to try to rescue Fina on his own, which was a super lame idea. *My plan was way better. He's going to get himself killed!*

"Why do men have to be so stubborn?" she asked Mr. Furface.

The cat simply stared up at her.

"All right. Let's get you a snack and some water." Perhaps along the way, she'd come up with another plan.

Who am I kidding? Mr. Gung Ho is going to try to be the hero. She knew the man. The need to protect and fight ran deep in his veins. He was complicated that way. *Decapitate your foe. Sure! Run headfirst into battle with a stick and some chewing gum, MacGyver style? Yep! Fix you a cup of chamomile and run you a bubble bath because you've had a very bad day because the bees are dying and you don't know why? You betcha! Knit a sweater for your hive because you have to go to Canada in the winter and try to help the bees who've caught the flu? Better believe it!*

Brutus *did* have a huge ego, but that was what made him so special. His ego was fueled by the need to serve others without regard for his image or what anyone thought. To him, tough meant something completely different compared to everyone else. Brutus would just as soon make you soup as he would disembowel your enemy. No difference to him.

Whichever woman landed him, whether it be Fina or some other, she would be the second luckiest woman on the planet. Colel was the first, in her mind. Her mate, Rys, was in many ways like Brutus, a selfless giver and tough as nails.

"All right! Let's get a move on!" she barked at her black-and-yellow army. "We need to think of something before Brutus ends up dead."

The swarm exited her hat and hovered in front of her face.

"Yes. Give me your ideas."

The bees conversed among themselves for a long moment before giving her their advice.

"No. You can't be serious."

They swarmed and riled. In all honesty, it was not her first choice, but maybe they were right.

"Well, you guys have always been a little crazy, but I don't see another option." Colel just hoped it wouldn't make things worse.

CHAPTER FOURTEEN

"I don't understand. I thought for sure we'd have tons of matches by now." Sitting outside on the deck of the plush guest bungalow overlooking the jagged red cliffs of Sedona, with his laptop and breakfast martini in hand, Zac scratched the side of his head. It was a crisp cool sunny morning, the day full of promise for turning the corner in this insane situation. Or so he thought.

He threw back his martini and set the empty glass to his side on the small wooden table. *Dammit. What did I do wrong?* The daily meeting with his brethren was in less than five minutes, and his plan to deliver a huge blow to the Universe's scheming had not panned out.

"It is okay, Mr. Zac." Tula appeared on the cedar lounge chair beside him, wearing a yellow sundress with white daisies and a high neckline. Her blonde locks were braided in two pigtails. She looked utterly delectable.

"You're back. I missed you."

"Yeah, I had to recharge a bit. Takes a lot out of me to materialize now." The sound of her voice dipped.

Fuuuck. She really was fading. And now, he was failing.

He blew out a long breath and closed his laptop. "No. It's not all right." This was supposed to work!

Russian babes!

Immortal men!

Boom! Sparks leading to salvation.

"I've failed again, Tula." He bowed his head and covered his face. "I can't seem to do anything right." *Except look really hot and tempt females. Okay, and men, too. And the occasional unicorn.*

"That's not true, my love," she said sympathetically. "You love me, and I couldn't ask for anything more right now."

He turned his head, the frustration bubbling over. "No, Tula. I have fucked everything up since day one. I wanted you because I couldn't have you. Then I needed you, but didn't think about what *you* needed. Then Cimil took you away because she knew I was too dense to see who you really were to me. I flipped and went to kill you, only to realize you were my mate, and ended up killing you anyway! On accident, yes, but what is an accident? Nothing more than a failure to see a potential outcome of one's actions." He groaned out a breath. "Cimil hid you from me because she knew how everything would turn out."

"What are you trying to say, Zac?" Tula whispered.

"I'm trying to say that…that…" His heart was

breaking. That he wanted to be with Tula more than he wanted to wear these black leather pants, in which he looked really cool. "I'm saying that every step of the way, Cimil has been right. Not 'right' in an obvious kind of way, but nonetheless, right. She said you would die if I pursued you. She said I would destroy you if I acted selfishly and tried to make you mine."

Tula's blue eyes filled with tears. "I-I don't understand. Are you...dumping me?"

"No, sweetheart. I would never dump you. But a man must recognize when he is defeated, when he doesn't have the answers." Zac exhaled. "I think for the first time in my existence, I must do what she says and leave you alone."

"Zac! No!"

"Tula, I've lost you more times than I can recall. And now I realize that if this was meant to be, if our love is meant to last, then I must stop intervening. I am only getting in the way!"

Tula looked at her tiny white flats. "I don't agree. Not even a little. But if that's the way you feel." She shrugged, clearly wounded.

"No, my love. It is not how I feel. Not even close. If it were up to me, you'd have your body; we'd be married and fucking nonstop for months. You'd be happy and laughing every day because that would be my one and only mission in life. But as it stands, I cannot have that. I cannot offer you that. Hell, I'm owned by a unicorn! And I must be man enough to recognize the truth."

She folded her arms over her chest. "Which is…?"

"I am a fool who has much to learn, and if I am smart, I will admit it. I need to get out of my own way and trust the Universe."

"The same Universe who put us in this place to begin with?"

"Yes. Because she's the one who brought you to me, and that makes her infinitely smarter."

"Fine." Tula huffed. "Then I guess this is good-bye."

"No. Never goodbye, Tula. All you need to do right now is conserve your energy and wait."

"For what? For the world to blow up?" She threw her arms to her sides.

"I will call for you. And when I do, it will be because this is all over and your body is waiting—I am waiting."

"I hope you're right."

He wouldn't dare promise her anything. It was his arrogance that had gotten them to this dire place.

"I hope so, too. I love you…" Tula disappeared right before his eyes.

Gods, I hope I'm right. Because the last time he'd listened to Cimil, he got into a lot of trouble. He'd ended up banished in the human world. On the other hand, getting in trouble had brought him to Tula.

ॐ ॐ

"Where is everyone?" Zac looked around the empty meeting hall, ready to play ball and stay out of his own way, but this wasn't what he had in mind.

He poked his head out into the long hallway that led to several offices and the elevators. Two human Uchben soldiers in black and gray camo strolled by.

"Hey, anyone seen my brethren?" Zac asked.

They shook their heads.

"Not for a few days, sir," said the tall one with cropped blond hair. "But I understand that three of the unmated gods are quarantined in our prison, and the others are all out on missions, leading the teams to round up the affected immortals."

Huh. Okay. I guess I missed that memo while I was at Club Minky. "How about Cimil? Seen her?"

"No, sir."

"Any idea where Gabrán is?" Gabrán was the Uchben chief and the one who would likely be coordinating communications with all the teams.

"He's quarantined, per Votan's orders."

Yes. Of course. All of their best immortal Uchben would be. For everyone's safety.

"How about Brutus?" Zac asked.

"Hasn't returned from his last mission, sir," answered the second man, shorter with black hair.

"Then who's running the show?" Zac asked.

The two soldiers exchanged awkward glances.

"No one? No one is running things?" Zac's eyes went wide.

"We're not sure. We went out last week to help with the efforts in New York City. We lost most of our men and had to retreat. We came back here with only the few vampires we'd managed to capture, and have been trying to scrounge up another team so we can go back out there."

This did not sound good. "How many soldiers have you found on the base?"

"Besides the ones in lockdown? None," replied the tall blond guy.

"None? Did you call the other bases? Italy? Hong Kong? Paris?"

"We put out alerts to everyone. None of the Uchben are answering. We assumed everyone's too busy to check in, or they're immortal and put themselves in quarantine in their own jails."

This was a disaster. They had many non-immortal humans in their Uchben army, but they were no match for crazy demigods, vampires, and other supernatural creatures who might have flipped. Without the aid of the immortal Uchben, the rest of their army was useless.

"Okay. I will go to the prison and see if anyone there has information." There had to be a few sane people in quarantine since many had been locked up as a precaution.

He was about to ask the two men to come with him, but to what purpose? If all of the gods and immortal soldiers were dead, flipped, or locked up, then they were all screwed. Two human soldiers wouldn't make one difference. "I hear there's a good movie on this afternoon at the mall—*The Gods Must Be Crazy*."

"We've already seen that one. The live performance. But thank you, sir. We'll be in the barracks." The two men walked off.

Zac headed in the other direction, feeling a cold, dark sensation creep over him. Goose bumps erupted on his skin the moment he stepped outside and started toward the entrance to their underground prison, which was separated from the rest of the compound and several stories down.

Something was definitely not right. *It's as if I can feel the evil vibes growing stronger. Like a giant festering boil about to pop.* He reached the heavy steel door and placed his palm on the scanner. The lock popped, and he stepped inside the small room to await the secure elevator down.

Zac scanned his hand a second time and poked the button. *Gods, why does this room feel so cold?* The elevator arrived and the doors slid open. He stepped inside and immediately noted an odd smell. Like…cotton candy or something sweet mixed with pot. *That's funny.*

He hit the button for the main prison floor about five stories down. As the elevator sank, the strange sensation grew stronger. Darkness. Evil. Rage. His body was being bombarded with all of them.

The doors slid open, and Zac felt his immortal heart slide down and grab his leg, quivering in terror.

"Dear Gods. Dear Gods. What is happening?"

Immortals of every kind were fighting, fucking, screaming, climbing the walls—literally. The sex fairies had several men tied up and were reciting bad poetry to them—at least it sounded bad to him, about flowers and fluffy bunnies and such. His brother K'ak was throwing lightning bolts at the vampires. Vampires were chewing on demigods. Demigods were strangling each other. Quite a few of the group were huddling in corners with iPhones and laptops, doing gods only knew what. "Who the hell gave them internet access?" Not a good idea.

"Zac!" His brother the God of Eclipses popped out of nowhere and pointed at him through the bars, his turquoise eyes glowing red. "There you are!"

Good thing there is a barrier between us. He did not look like he was in a nice mood.

Zac poked the call button for the elevator just as a loud crash exploded near the barred door.

Zac looked over his shoulder. His other brother K'ak was throwing bolts of electricity at the lock. *Oh no. They're going to get out!*

The elevator chimed. He stepped inside and pressed the button for the ground floor. *Hurry. Hurry!* He could see the inmates almost had the lock open.

The elevator doors slid shut. Once he arrived, he hopped out and started looking for something to shut off the elevator. Any second now, the creatures, three gods, and other possessed immortals would start pouring out of the prison.

He noticed a little door to the side of the room. Inside were some cleaning supplies and paint.

Ah! The emergency shutoff! It was a switch on the wall.

He flipped it and grabbed the black paint.

He popped off the lid and with his fingers wrote on the wall beside the elevator doors:

Do not enter! Danger! Turn back now!

"I don't think we're so dangerous. Hehehe…"

Zac turned his head to find three red-eyed sex fairies fluttering at eye level. They were usually beautiful, and yes, sexy, little creatures adept at the arts of pleasure, but these ones looked like they'd sooner eat your face than sit on it.

They must have flown upstairs through the elevator shaft. Zac really needed to talk to Votan about the prison security.

The larger fairy, about the size of a football, flashed a set of gleaming white teeth. "And I think we'll be turning that elevator back on." She flew into the closet and flipped the switch before turning back to him.

"As for you!" She pointed her sharp little claw at him. "I think it's time we show the God of Temptation a few tricks."

Something hit him on the back of the head, and the world went dark.

CHAPTER FIFTEEN

For two straight days, Brutus had been following the group of nine women, including Fina as their prisoner, through some of the wettest, darkest rainforest he'd ever seen. Whatever route they were taking back to the village, it was ten times tougher than the way they'd traveled before. The vegetation was so dense that the trees almost entirely blocked out the sunlight. Adding to his strife, he had no plan, no weapons, and no idea how he was going to take on all of these female warriors, but he knew he had to do something before they reached their village. It was far easier to fight eight women than ninety-eight. Sadly, however, the only thing he could think of was to wait until one of the women fell behind or separated herself from the group. Then he could overpower her, take her sword, and wait. When the other women came looking for the missing member of the group, he would take them out, too. He'd hardly call it a great plan, given how it was dependent upon the women only coming at him two or three at a time.

Another problem: Those women were freaking machines! They didn't stop to eat, pee, or sleep more than a few hours each night. He was keeping up with them, but barely. And fighting anyone in such a weakened state was not wise.

Tonight, I must make my move. If he waited any longer, he would be too sleep deprived and hungry to rescue a flea, let alone his princess.

Wait. My *princess?* That was odd. Fina wasn't his. She was…just a very hot, strong, smart, and loyal warrior.

Sure, he admired her. Sure, he wouldn't mind a little swordplay in her bed, but he didn't want a relationship with the damned woman. Going after her was merely the right thing to do.

Just around midnight, the women finally stopped to rest and build a fire to roast some lizards and squirrels he assumed they'd caught along the way.

Hiding behind a large tree, Brutus's stomach grumbled. What he wouldn't give for a pizza or a burger and fries. He'd been trying to eat healthier these past few months, because immortal or not, his body felt stronger when he ate nutritious natural foods, but right now he could go for some serious junk food. *Or even squirrel.*

As the women ate, he snuck around the perimeter of their camp to get a better lay of the land. Fina was about twenty feet from the fire, tied to a tree. Two women were tending to the jungle kabobs. Four women were eating.

Hmm. I wonder where the other two are.

"Hello, handsome. Back for some more fun?" He felt a sharp spear between his shoulder blades.

He turned to fight, but he felt something scratch his arm. *Oh no. It's that poison Colel mentioned.* His vision turned blurry, and then something hit him on the back of the head.

"Great. We're back in the village," Brutus mumbled when he came to, realizing just how badly his "plan" had failed. Both he and Fina were tied to wooden posts about five feet apart on the very same beach where there'd been a bonfire the night they escaped.

I love repeating life's worst moments. So magical. At least there was no cauldron this time, but the early morning air held a stillness that gave him the heebie-jeebies anyway.

"Fina!" he whispered loudly. Her head was slumped over, and she wasn't moving. From this angle, she didn't appear to be injured—no blood or bruises—and her chest was rising with her breath, so that was good news.

"Fina!" he tried again.

She stirred a bit and began snoring. The sound was awful, but it was kind of cute the way her little lips puckered and her eyelids fluttered when she slept. He wondered what she might be dreaming about. Him? Or better even, the two of them in the throes of ecstasy.

"Well, well, well! Look who's awake." Wearing nothing more than a brown burlap sarong, her blonde hair in a braid down her back, Helga sneered at him. Her eyes were fixed on his leaf skirt, which had dried out. There was a grassy teepee over his lap.

"Don't flatter yourself, Oh-Mighty-Crotch-Ogler of the Jungle. The General is not saluting you and never will. So forget about it," he growled.

Helga huffed. "Don't worry. I wouldn't dare dishonor our sacred land by lying with a lowly *man* upon it."

Well, that was good news.

Helga took out her knife and crouched in front of him, pointing the tip at his nose. "But I wouldn't mind taking a snack."

His stomach rolled. These women were animals.

"Helga, back the fuck off. You know the rules. He is not to be touched until the cleansing ritual," Fina grumbled with a groggy voice, coming out of her sleep.

"Then maybe I should take a piece of you." Helga stood and pointed her blade at Fina.

"Just be sure you have the queen's permission first," Fina said, "because I'm sure she has very specific and very painful plans for me. You wouldn't want to ruin them by pre-maiming me."

"Right you are, Fina." Helga snickered. "In fact, you're both slated to die within the hour. Your mother and the others are gathered at the wisdom tree at this very moment, trying to decide who will have the honor of slicing your necks." She flashed a sinister grin, her dark eyes protruding from her head as she marched off.

"What a charming woman." Brutus let out a sigh of relief. "Nice to see you awake. Are you all right?"

"Ummm…" Fina wiggled her ass in the sand, trying to straighten out her back. "Besides having my hands going numb behind my back, and my neck aching like a sonofabitch because I had to carry you for the last ten miles of the journey here, I'm fantastic."

She carried him? He probably outweighed her by fifty or sixty pounds. Pure muscle, of course. It was pretty hot knowing she could carry him.

Fina tilted back her head and moved it side to side, giving her neck a crack before shooting a snarl his way. "Oh. And by the way, I really love the part about sacrificing my life for you, and both of us ending up here. About to die. That's really wonderful."

"I'm very sorry. This was not my intention." He'd never failed on a mission before, and it shamed him that this was the first time.

She shrugged and looked out at the hypnotic blues and greens of the roaring waterfall. "Yeah, well, word of advice: The next time someone gives up their life for you, just send a thank you note or something instead of trying to be the hero."

"Don't get me wrong," he said, "I'm grateful that you would do such a thing for me, but I would like to point out that had you consulted me first, you would have known I'd never allow you to sacrifice your life for mine."

She looked away, but didn't speak.

"Why did you do it?" he asked.

She remained silent.

"I'm assuming we are both going to die this fine morning, so what have you got to lose by telling me? We both might as well leave this earth without regrets and not as cowards."

She met his gaze again and narrowed her dark eyes. He loved how intense she was.

"All right. Let's see how brave *you* are," she said. "Why did *you* come after *me*?"

The strong emotions stirred inside him—feelings he hadn't permitted to see the light of day until now. But it was time to deal with the truth, no matter how uncomfortable. After all, wasn't that what good warriors did? They confronted fear, not walked away from it.

"If you must know, I find you very attractive," he said bluntly. "And, well, I admire your loyalty and intelligence."

"So, basically, you want to screw me." She frowned.

He gave that some thought. "Yes. If I'm being completely honest, I would very much like that."

"Yeah, well, sorry, but I'm not the casual-sex,

one-night-stand sort of woman."

He nodded. "I am aware."

"And so you came after me, hoping for what?"

He shrugged. "To see if Colel was right."

"About what?" she snapped.

"If you recall, Colel mentioned that if I let go of her, I would fall for someone else."

Fina didn't frown this time. In fact, there was a hopeful warmth in her eyes. "And?"

"I was wondering if that person might be you." He held his gaze steady on her face. She needed to know he meant what he said. This might be his last day on earth, and he wanted no regrets. *What a shame it would be if she didn't know the truth.*

She stared for a long moment and was about to speak, but then clamped her mouth shut and stared down at her lap.

He couldn't tell if she was flattered or thought he was ridiculous.

"Your turn," he said. "Why did you fake that broken ankle?"

She toggled her head from side to side. "I figured Zeus would have a better chance of escaping if I gave myself up."

"You sacrificed yourself for your cat? Sure. Okay." He chuckled bitterly. "I know that's not true because you admitted you did it for me." That was what sparked this very conversation.

"Fine. I did it because I think you're hot and maybe I admire you, too."

Really? "So then why not stay with me? Why not keep running?" he asked.

"I guess…I guess, I saw the way you looked at the bee lady, and I knew there wasn't room in your heart for anyone else—me specifically. Also, you were getting tired and slowing down. I didn't see the point in all of us getting caught when the trackers really wanted me."

Brutus's heart accelerated, his pulse like thunder in his ears. *She's so damned hot.* Fina had the spirit of a warrior. She knew that sometimes one had to make sacrifices for others. It took a brave person to be so selfless. Heroism wasn't always about running headfirst into battle or fighting wars. Being a hero was about duty—to your family, friends, tribe, team, and companion animals. Sometimes it meant simply being there to draw a bubble bath. Sometimes it meant cooking a meal. And sometimes it meant running after a woman you admire and desire when you know in the back of your mind that you have no chance of winning her.

"I did not want you to die alone," he mumbled, realizing why he'd truly gone after her. "I think you are far too special to leave this world not knowing how beautiful, brave, and smart you are. And," he inhaled deeply, "even if I don't really know you, I believe you could have healed my broken heart and taken the place of Colel."

Fina's big brown eyes watered up, and she cuss-ed—or at least he thought she had. He didn't recognize the language, but her words sounded pained.

"Did I say something wrong?" he asked. "I only meant to be honest and—"

"No," Fina sniffled. "I'm crying because I've dreamed of this moment a thousand times. I never saw the face or envisioned being tied to a post, about to die, but I dreamed of this feeling in my heart." She smiled softly. "Thank you, Brutus. Thank you for saying the perfect words before I die." She sighed contentedly.

The fact that Fina found such joy in his words made him feel particularly proud. He'd finally become *her* hero. It meant everything to him.

Feeling exceptionally brave, he asked, "What do you think our children would have been like?"

Fina gave him an odd look and then laughed. "Yeah. Sure. Why not?" She inhaled deeply. "Since I'm only capable of having female children, I think the first one would have your build—tall, strong, able to crack a coconut with her ass."

Brutus grinned smugly. He did have a mighty ass.

Fina went on, "And the second child would grow up to be my size—lean and muscular like a jaguar."

He liked the idea of having two girls: one fast, one strong. "And their hair? Would they have your lovely streak of gold?"

"Hmmm...I kind of hope not, because it's the

sign of our leader, and I think I would want my daughters to grow up in the modern world, making their own way, making their own decisions."

"So you do not agree with your village's way of life?"

"No! Gods no!" She laughed. "Everyone is miserable and angry all the time. Probably because our kind needs sex. A lot of it."

"I did notice your people have a lot of pent-up sexual frustration."

"We are very in touch with our bodies," she said, "which means our senses are heightened, and we run hot. And since we're all related—cousins, aunts, sisters, etc.—it's not like there's any hanky-panky going on between us. Mittens is about the only game in town."

Mittens? I don't want to know. "So the lack of sex is something you'd change if you were leader. What else?"

"Where to start?" she chirped bitterly. "No one gets a say in their education or running the village. We're told which jobs we do, and it's usually hunting, building, or patrolling. So that means the artists, the weavers, and the ones who love music must practice in secret. They fear for their lives. Also, most of us do not enjoy eating people. That's just gross, but we're forced to do everything Mother says. Honestly, it's oppressive. We're warriors, strong-willed and strong-minded. We have been bred to think for ourselves, yet we're treated like children. So, yeah, when you ask if I agree with this way of life? I can confidently say that I don't. If I were given the chance to be leader, that's what I would do. Lead. Not rule."

Brutus nodded. She truly was perfect. Selfless, strong, intelligent, and very, very beautiful. The most beautiful thing of all was the fact she was oblivious to just how sexy she was.

"Well, since we are not going to have the chance to live out our destinies, I would like to say that I think you would have been an incredible leader. And mother to our two strong girls. And wife." He grinned. "I would have enjoyed deflowering you, getting you pregnant, and fucking you repeatedly throughout our very long lives."

Her cheeks flushed, and he could see her breathing accelerate with the rise of her chest. "So tell me, what would you have done our first time?"

Oh, she wanted to go there, did she?

He was game.

After all, they had minutes left to live. Why not spend them thinking of enjoyable things?

"Well." He cleared his throat and straightened his back against the post, trying to get comfortable for this little round of sexting. Without the phones, of course. "I would definitely start out by taking you to my home in Sedona. It is a very cozy adobe atop a hill, looking out across red cliffs and miles of beautiful desert. And since there is an incredible sunset each night, where the sky bursts into hot pinks and blazing reds, I would set out a very nice bottle of wine and a blanket on my patio. We would watch the sunset and enjoy the majestic beauty of nature—"

"That sounds super romantic, but I don't know when my mother is coming to remove my head, so could you skip to the sex part, please?"

He grinned. "Okay, then, I would take you inside, remove your clothing. I would tell you that I was going to lick and kiss you from head to toe, but by the time I got done sucking one of your nipples and found your entrance wet and ready, I wouldn't be able to stop myself from pinning your hands over your head and taking you hard. Like a savage beast."

Fina bit her lower lip, her pupils dilating. "How hard?"

"You'd scream my name and claw at my back."

"Because you're big," she muttered, her voice dreamy.

Mmm... Now she was catching on. "Yes. You've felt my hard cock in your hands. You know how big." Just thinking about how good her hand had felt on his shaft was making his cock thicken at this very moment. One little brush of a leaf and the General would be saluting all over the dirt in front of him.

"I have," she admitted. "And I've imagined how good it would feel inside me."

"It would feel *very* good," he purred in a deep, low voice. "I would push myself deep and show your wet pussy no mercy. And when I was done with you, I'd flip you over and fuck you again. I'd leave your skin bathed in sweat, every muscle limp with contentment. You'd be so spent, I'd have to carry you to the tub for a long soak, so I could ravage you again an hour later."

"Mmmm…" She closed her eyes, a sensual grin dancing on her lips. "I am so wet right now."

"I am so hard right now." He closed his eyes, too, soaking in the sexual heat wafting in the air between them. "If I were untied, nothing would stop me from taking you to your hut and—"

"I would never allow my bloodline to be defiled on sacred land by a *male*," said a sharp female voice.

Brutus opened his eyes and saw a woman standing there in a rainbow caftan. She had dark eyes and a blonde streak on her right temple. Unlike her daughter, the queen was heinous looking with scars all over her face. *Probably was attacked by her own mirror for being such a shrew.*

"Queen Caca." Brutus felt his tire deflate instantly. "Lovely to see you again." He dipped his head. "As always, your hospitality is phenomenal. Might I suggest opening a bed-and-breakfast for those who enjoy an oppressive vibe?"

"Shut up, you fool," the queen growled.

"Why don't *you* shut up, Mother," Fina snarled.

"How dare you speak to me in that manner." The queen pointed a bony finger at Fina.

Damn, woman, clean your fingernails once in a

while. They were caked with grime.

"I'll speak to you any way I like," Fina threw back. "I'm going to die, and I might as well get some things off my chest." Fina looked directly at Brutus. "Right? I mean, I already have my husband, the most incredible sex of my life, and two wonderful girls. The only thing missing is for you to take a flying fuck off a cliff so that our people are free of your archaic bull crap."

Brutus couldn't help beaming at his fantasy wife. Their little game of make-believe was suddenly more real to him than anything. It was a feeling in his heart. Passion, love, a home. In an instant, Fina was all that and more, simply because he'd allowed himself to imagine this different life. A good life. With her.

Colel had been right; all he had to do was let go, and the bond would break. In an instant, his heart had been filled with something infinitely more powerful: A woman he chose on his own.

A woman who wants me, freely, as much as I want her. It dawned on him that this relationship had not been thrust upon him by the Universe, which went perfectly with his independent, noble spirit. Like a bolt of electricity to the spine, that shot up into his brain, he could see it all so clearly now. The perfect woman had to be *his* choice. And had it not been for being mated to Colel first, he might have met Fina and always wondered if there was another woman out there, about to be sprung on him by the

Universe.

Now I have no doubts.
And she's sitting right beside me.
About to die.

He couldn't sit idly by and do nothing. He wanted them to have their chance, to make these fantasies in their heads become real. Yes, it was a sudden turn of events, but he'd been around long enough to know when something was a lie and when it was not.

The queen snapped her fingers at one of the women standing in the group behind her, holding the holy battle-ax. "Time for talk is over."

The woman hesitated, gripping the weapon firmly in her hand, a scowl on her face.

What had Fina said to him the other day? About how he had been so wrapped up in his mission that he'd failed to assess the situation.

His eyes darted over the faces in the crowd. The woman gripping the battle-ax wasn't the only one glaring at the queen. The scent of defiance was in the air, and he suspected all they needed was a spark to ignite it.

"You know," he spoke up, "I have worked for the gods for centuries, including with Cimil. I have been a lowly soldier. I have been a leader. I have been a trusted member of their very dysfunctional family. And if there is one thing I have learned, it's that leaders, the ones worth remembering and idolizing, are not swinging the biggest swords. They are the ones who offer their swords. They serve selflessly. They believe there is no higher purpose than to use their gifts to help others. They love their people and only want to see them thrive and reach their full potential. In my experience, fear, force, and hate are the tools of the weak-minded. They are used by those not worthy of following." Brutus raised his chin high, thinking of his men, who would follow him to the ends of the earth and whom he'd give his life for. Bonds like that were not forged in the muddy depths of power trips and insecurity. They were the product of genuine respect, for one's self and for others. Dare he say love, too. In a very platonic, brotherly way. "A good leader is given power by their people. They don't take it with force or use fear to keep it."

"Silence! I've heard enough!" The queen marched over and reached for the battle-ax, but the tribeswoman refused to give it up.

"You can silence Fina and me," Brutus said, "but then everyone here will know that you fear the truth. You fear that Fina might be loved, and you'll be left out in the cold."

"I fear nothing except weakness!" the queen yelled, veins popping from her scarred forehead. "I have seen what happens when we allow it into our village. The men come. They take what they want. They rape and kill. They take us as slaves. So while you might have the modern notions of kindness and love, I am *not* so naïve. And that is why I am leader."

"Okay, Mother," Fina finally jumped in. "Then that basically means you think we need *you* to survive—that we're all a bunch of stupid, incapable children instead of the brave, strong women we really are. So if you hate weakness so much, then you must hate us, since we all *need* you so much." Her words were ripe with sarcasm. "I mean, that certainly is how you treat us, is it not? You punish us, deprive us of love, you make sure there is no joy in our lives. Because we are disgustingly weak, and our sense of purpose should come only from pleasing you.

"So in light of that, and how beneath you we are, I suggest the following: Those who feel they need you to survive and are *sooo* afraid of living without you can stay. The rest may go and remove themselves and all their nasty weakness from your view."

Yes! Brutus cheered on the inside. Fina had backed Chaca-caca-whatever into a corner, and it was a damned bright one that illuminated the queen's true colors.

The queen lifted her chin. "I think what's really going on is that you're afraid to die, Fina. I mean," she chuckled sadistically, "we all know how you freed Brutus here because you were too squeamish to watch him die. And then you ran away. Like the weak coward you are."

Brutus booed on the inside. "Helping innocent

people makes her a merciful and strong woman. Weak is the person who needs control." He'd seen such people a million times. They needed to poke the bear, stab the bear, hurt the bear, all to hear the bear cry so that they might feel some semblance of power. The bear's cry made them feel like they existed. But hurting innocent people only made you an asshole. It made you a bully. "Fina is a woman whose power comes from within. It is why she's unafraid to show mercy and kindness, even if it means defying a frigid, closed-minded, coldhearted bitch."

"Ohhh…snap!" the women around them all crooned.

"I'd follow a coldhearted bitch any day over a soft, whiny, spoiled little princess." Helga stepped forward, a large sword in hand. "Fina is nothing but a cavity in the mouth of the voice of true greatness, and I say it's time for us to extract the decay, so that our queen may bed a man immediately and make a replacement heir." Helga pointed her sword directly at Brutus. "And I think this fine specimen will do. He is, after all, strong and healthy. His mind is weak, easily swayed by pussy, but he's no different from all men."

If Fina's eyes were fighter planes, she would be shooting Helga with missiles.

Helga spun in a circle, staring down her tribeswomen. "Sisters, let me remind you what happened the last time anyone challenged the queen."

The group of tall blonde women grumbled and exchanged muted side conversations.

Brutus didn't know the significance of this event Helga spoke of, but if he wanted to make a counter-argument, he had to ask: "For those of us who weren't there, enlighten us. I for one would like to know what was so horrible that you would keep this joy-sucking tyrant in place rather than follow someone like Fina."

Helga snickered. "I bet you'd like to know, but we don't answer to you, *male*."

"Cimil." Fina groaned. "Cimil came along. She said if we didn't listen to Mother and obey her, we would all be taken to the underworld and forced to live out eternity as slaves to her monkeys."

Monkeys? "There are no monkeys in the under-world," Brutus scoffed.

"Well, not yet!" a shrill, horribly familiar voice called out.

Brutus turned his head to see bright red hair in pigtails. *Cimil.* And she was wearing a tent. Not a dress or muumuu, but a real-life tent with the poles and zippers and everything. Kind of like an old-fashioned hoop skirt, but this covered her from the neck down and was significantly larger.

The women gasped and fell to the ground, averting their eyes. Everyone except him, Fina, and the queen.

"Cimil…" Brutus growled. "I hope you're here to rescue us and tell these women there are no monkeys in the underworld."

Cimil marched over, careful to step on absolutely everyone and make them yelp as she passed by. "There are no monkeys in the underworld. I made it all up so you'd all listen to Chaca Chica here. And now you should all let Brutus and Fina go so they can get it on." Cimil looked at Brutus. "There. Happy now?" Cimil held out her hands.

"But, but why would you lie like that—about the monkeys?" Fina asked.

"Because I'm evil, which everyone knows. And, ultimately, my lies were going to make you a more resilient leader, Fina. But now my plans are shot to hell because the world as we know it is ending in about seventy-two hours. May I go now?" Cimil patted her stomach. "Because I've got a load of babies to drop, and I'd like to do so in my bouncy castle, surrounded by family so we can all die in a fiery ball of doom together."

The tribeswomen exchanged glances.

Brutus just sat there, obviously, his heart and soul telling him one unified: *Cimil actually sounds serious for once.*

Was it possible? Was Cimil actually telling the damned truth? Because he generally knew when she was lying. He could see it in her face—all part of his honed skills as a soldier engaging with a very dangerous foe.

"Well?" Cimil tapped her pink fuzzy slipper, still looking directly at him.

"Well what?" Brutus asked.

"Are you happy now? Because Colel made me promise I couldn't leave until I paid back that favor I owed her—she loaned me a truck full of honey for a wrestling match with Big Foot. Anywhoodles, I seriously do not want to die with a debt hanging over my head. Those types go into the Pit of Gorg and can't come out until they've matched all of the Tupperware lids to the containers, which basically means you stay forever."

Huh? He had so, sooo many questions, but he couldn't pass up this opportunity to save his "wife."

"If you untie us," he said, "and take Fina and me away from here to Sedona, then I'll be happy."

"Hey. What about us?" one woman piped up. "You said we'd get to choose."

Brutus looked at Cimil. "And you must take anyone who wishes to go, too."

Cimil rolled her bright turquoise eyes. "Fine. But just warning you, your virgin ears and eyes might not be prepared for the things going down at the Uchben headquarters, so stay far, far away from that place. Unless you plan on flipping, in which case, you should definitely go because it's wild and perfect for evil people."

Brutus stared, now more worried than ever. Niccolo, his dog, was at the compound, being looked after by one of his men. He hoped? "Where is Colel?"

"She said something about her bees going nuts

and having to drop off some man named Gato. Guess she got tired of Rys."

Oh no. Her bees had flipped, too? Their connection was incredibly strong. There wasn't a place on this planet where they couldn't find her.

He looked over at Fina, and the two locked eyes. His urge to rescue Colel was still there, still embedded deep inside him.

"It's okay," Fina said reassuringly. "I know you have to go to her."

He did have to go because it was what he did when he was needed. He showed up when no one else would.

He was about to tell Fina he'd be back, that he'd find her later once Colel was safe, but... *What if there are no more laters?*

"I am sorry, Fina, but I am needed," he said. "I hope you understand."

"I figured." The disappointment on her face was well masked, but there was no mistaking the hardness in her eyes—the sign of a warrior sucking up "the suck."

"Good. Because my destiny is deflowering a princess and enjoying every moment together."

Her eyes lit up and her mouth flashed the most gorgeous smile.

"All right, you two lovebirds. Time to go. The ticks are tocking." Cimil untied him. Brutus got up and ran to Fina, releasing her arms. Chaka and Cimil began arguing over the whole thing, basically the queen saying she would have Cimil's head for this betrayal, and Cimil saying she was a goddess and could do anything she liked. "So there. Suck it."

The moment Fina was up, Brutus was on her—arm banded around her waist, pulling her smaller lean body to him. He gazed into her dark eyes, savoring every drop, every ounce of the moment, and dipped his head. Just as their lips were about to touch, he stopped.

"What?" she asked.

The feelings he had earlier were real—the craving in his heart, the fire in his loins, the sense of knowing there was no finer woman on the planet. But if he kissed her now, he wouldn't be able to stop, and this was not the place he wanted to deflower her. She deserved so much better. She deserved to have her feelings respected and her every desire delivered on, which he hoped included showing her a little disrespect in the bedroom with some dirty, dirty sex. If the world was truly coming to an end, why not? Why not make the dream they'd shared into a reality? *Carpe diem*, and all that.

Brutus got down on one knee. "Fina, you once said you owned me, and I would like to own you back. Will you marry me?"

She raised two dark brows. "Are you being serious right now?"

"You said you were not the sort of woman to engage in casual sex. You said you cared who you invited into your bed and whose seed you allowed into your womb—or something like that." Not the exact words she used, but close enough. "I want you very badly, but I also want you to know you mean more to me than the savage animalistic fuckathon I have secretly desired from the first moment you stroked my cock."

Fina gave him an odd look. "Umm…that's possibly the nicest, sweetest thing anyone has ever said to me."

"Is that a yes?" he asked, because the ticks were tocking, according to Cimil.

"Yes." She smiled so brightly, it made his heart ache.

He stood and pushed his lips to her cheek.

She recoiled. "My cheek? But…"

"But nothing," he whispered in her ear. "If I kiss you, I'm in you. And I want our first time to be perfect."

She pulled back and beamed up at him. "Okay, then. No kissing."

"Excellent."

"But do you mind if I rub one out with Mittens?" she asked.

He crinkled his nose. "Yes." Because…well, what the fuck was a Mittens?

"Just thought I'd ask." Fina shrugged.

Brutus grabbed her hand. "Come on, let's get out of here."

"How exactly?"

"Does it matter?" Walking, running, flying on Cimil's horny unicorn. Anything was better than here.

She squeezed his hand. "No."

CHAPTER SIXTEEN

Turned out that Cimil had come prepared for once, but as usual, her methods reached the extremes. Since all of the healthy soldiers and vampires were busy, Cimil had called in a favor from her nanny to get her to the jungle quickly and get the rest of their party to the aircraft carrier.

For anyone not in the know, her nanny was a Maaskab, an evil Mayan priest who excelled in the dark arts. On the surface, it sounded like a terrible option for child care; however, the Maaskab were the first to flip, and being supremely evil meant that they were temporarily the nicest people on the planet. Her nanny was no exception. Quite literally, he was the "give you the dried-human-skin sarong right off his lower torso" kind of guy. Since that was about all they wore. Sort of like a diaper made of people hide. They also favored necklaces made from the thumbs of their foes and didn't believe in bathing since they covered their bodies in a mixture of dried blood and soot made from black jade—a very powerful substance with all sorts of magical properties.

Anyway, Cimil's nanny called a few friends to

clear a nice spot in the jungle so they could land helicopters and get everyone to an Uchben personnel carrier.

Honestly, Brutus was impressed. For the first time ever, Cimil was all business, which, of course, made him worry.

Brutus found spare fatigues for himself and gray camo blankets for the ninety-three ladies who'd joined them on the plane. Cimil and her nanny were up front flying. Probably not the best idea, but he was rusty operating such aircraft, and Cimil flew all the time, so she said.

I wonder if she just meant she rides Minky a lot. Oh well, no use worrying about it now, right? He and Fina were free. The queen's evil reign was over. Now he had bigger things to worry about. For example, figuring out why Cimil was insisting the world was coming to an end. Again. And he believed her. Generally, there was a sparkle of pure evil joy when she told them it was the end of the world. This time? Nothing.

Also, during a quick side conversation with Cimil, she'd said there weren't enough mated couples to round up and quarantine the affected immortals. *Nothing new.* It was the reason he'd come on this mission to begin with. But now Cimil said the evil vibes of the immortals were rubbing off on humans, because the immortals were running around getting inside everyone's heads.

There must be a way to stop this. He wondered

why the plague even began in the first place. The gods believed the Universe enjoyed keeping everyone on their toes, but why would she want to end her biggest source of entertainment? *Just doesn't make sense.*

This whole thing started right after the last apocalypse—when evil vampires and the Maaskab tried to take over the world. The good guys won, of course, but after the dust settled, there were some major wartime shenanigans to address. Cimil and Zac were at the top of the list of shenanihooligans and were banished to the human world for their many misdeeds. Their sentence included having to match up one hundred single immortals, which was supposed to teach them about love and compassion—something the two lacked. But right away, this new plague hit, and everyone assumed it was simply more of the Universe's scheming.

What if the Universe had nothing to do with this plague? *I know we're missing something. Something obvious.* A plague was a disease, and diseases had to start somewhere. A point of origin. Also, there was a vaccine of sorts (being mated and/or in love), which meant the Universe really couldn't be out to end the world. If she wanted to end things, she wouldn't give them all a cure. She'd send an incurable, horrible flesh-eating virus that would wipe out everyone.

Hmmm... I wonder what Fina thinks. She was smart, and she was a student of Mother Nature, very attuned to her surroundings.

He glanced over at Fina, who stood talking and laughing with several of her sisters. The plane's engines were too loud for him to hear their conversation, but it was nice to see her happy. She had her family back. Well, some of them. The queen had stayed behind with a few of her superfans, like Helga. They could die in a viper pit for all he cared.

Still wearing her insanely hot black suede bikini, Fina came over and sat next to him on the long bench that ran the length of the cargo area.

"So, looks like things have been smoothed over with your tribeswomen, yes?" he asked.

Fina shrugged with a happy little smile. "Yeah. I guess so. But you know the best part?"

"What?" he asked.

"They can't wait to meet your men!"

"Really?"

"Yep. Every one of them wants, and I quote, 'their own Brutus' to ride nightly."

At this stage of the game, mating his men might be a moot point in terms of solving the plague, but who was he to stand in anyone's way if they sought love?

"Well, then, we will have to devise a plan to get them paired up." He explained how the prison was packed with singles right now. Perhaps the most efficient way would be to allow the women to enter, one by one, and see if any of the men reacted.

"This is so exciting! I'm going to tell them

now." Fina slid her hand into his and gave it a squeeze.

Tingles instantly spiked up his arm. He jerked his hand back.

"What's the matter?" Fina asked.

He leaned in a little closer, speaking out of the side of his mouth. "It seems that merely touching you is rousing my soldier."

Fina sighed. "Mine, too. I think we should just get this over with. I mean, what if the plane crashes or something happens and we don't make it to your house? I'm all for our fantasy and things being perfect our first time together, but I'm also pragmatic."

Just the thought of being inside her made his pants uncomfortably snug. They were already a size too small.

He tried to adjust himself, but it only made his manhood harder by touching it.

Fina looked down at his camo tent. "Well, looks like someone agrees with me."

"No. I'm not going to plow you here on a plane, in front of all these people."

Fina shrugged. "Nothing they haven't seen before."

He knew what sorts of things these ladies were comfortable with. Sharing. Nudity. Sex while others rated them—about half the women had brought friends to watch when he'd been tied to that tree. He had nothing to hide, but it was a little odd when they started holding up signs with numbers. Mostly eights and nines. A few tens, too. He wanted Fina's first time to be a ten. And he wanted it to be private. What he felt for her was special and should be treated so. In fact, had he known from the beginning who she really was—his destiny—he would have fought tooth and nail to keep her tribe off him. Going forward, however, there would never be another. Just her. Only her. Even when he jerked off. *I'm such a romantic.*

"Let us get some rest. When we wake, we'll be in Arizona." And with some sleep, he hoped his superior brain might produce the answer to his question: How did this plague really begin?

"What if there is no one there to marry us?" she asked.

"Then…we'll cross that bridge when we get there." He knew a few humans who were ordained and could get the job done.

Brutus grabbed a blanket and found a free spot against the wall that separated the cargo hold from the cockpit. He sat down on the floor and leaned against it, patting the spot beside him in an invitation to Fina.

She smiled and came over. "You really just want to sleep?"

"Yes." He was a man on a new mission. And he wanted to start this relationship like he started any mission. Everything had to be perfectly planned. Only then would victory be assured.

≳ ⚶

Fina had never felt so happy. Overnight, her life had gone from a never-ending nightmare of doom, where nothing ever changed with her mother, to this! Yes, Cimil claimed the world was going to hell in a handbasket, but there was something about the goddess she couldn't trust.

For starters, Fina's tribe had lived in a state of angry celibacy and practiced mannibalism for centuries all because this bat-shit-crazy redhead showed up one day and told them to do it.

Fast-forward to this morning, and it was all a giant crock.

Who does that?

Fina went over to tell her sisters the good news regarding how to find them men when they arrived. It was better they knew the plan, because she herself would be indisposed.

Fina returned to Brutus, who'd passed out, slumped against the wall with a blanket over him. Poor man looked exhausted.

She sat next to him and stretched the blanket over her body, but the moment the edges of their bodies touched, she felt that spark. A warm sensual heat ran from the top of her head down to her toes. Along the way, it made her nipples perk and the space between her thighs throb. *Mmmm…*

She turned her head and studied his gorgeous features—the heart-shaped lips and strong jaw, the thick brow line and inky stubble. His beauty was rugged and masculine, his body was enormous and strong, but at the same time, he had a gentle side and wasn't afraid to show it. Also, he was hung. So that was nice.

She slid her hand under the blanket and found his cock pressing against his pants. She'd only meant to give it a pat—as if to say "you're mine now"—but touching him only aroused her more.

She unzipped him and took his length in her hand. Perhaps he wouldn't mind if she gave them both some pleasure. Not sex. Just an appetizer.

The lights were dim in the cargo hold. Everyone was falling asleep now anyway. Mittens, the ever vigilant, ever invisible guardian of her tribe, was off in the corner napping or reading or doing whatever invisible Mittens did on planes. She knew he was there, though. Mittens always made the air around him just a bit warmer.

I can't wait to introduce him to Brutus. Everything had happened so fast that she never got the chance. Also, introducing the creature took a little finesse—some offerings of cricket ears and maybe a little goat meat. After that, she and Brutus could get on with their new life.

Fina smiled devilishly. She was a hunter, a fighter, a woman with urges who'd waited centuries for this—for him. And her days of being told what to do were over. Very over.

I take what I want. And I want him.

She slid one hand down her pants and with her other hand began stroking him. He groaned and mumbled her name but remained asleep.

She closed her eyes and imagined his hot dick sliding into her, pushing against her walls, and going deep. She imagined riding him hard and him coming inside her. *Oh, yes…*

Fina felt the climax instantly building. Whatever this thing was between them, it produced a potent erotic energy. It was like they were meant to fuck. And fight. And live out their lives in one wild adventure.

Brutus began moving his hips as she stroked him faster beneath the blanket, but she wanted to watch him explode in her hand while she came. She moved the blanket aside, so only she had a little view, and then went to work.

So close. So close. She felt the heat building and then… *Yes! Yes!* The wave of ecstasy hit hard, pulling her up and out of her body, just as Brutus's cock erupted. His brow line shrugged, and he let out a hard breath.

"Oh, Colel…" he groaned.

Colel? Fucking Colel? Fina snapped her hand away lest she be tempted to rip off his manhood. *That sonofabitch! Colel?* He was dreaming of the bee lady?

Fina put his cock away, wiped her hand on the corner of the blanket, and got up. In this moment, she wanted to kick that smug, sleepy grin off his fucking face!

Fina went into the small bathroom to wash up. She hadn't seen this coming—no pun intended—but she should have. *I'm so ridiculous.* Colel had been Brutus's mate. His mate! She'd seen the way he looked at the tall, statuesque blonde—with those perfect perky tits and long legs.

I am a fool to think he could switch it off and just want me, only me, a handful of hours later.

While her mother might be a loon, perhaps she had been right about one thing: Men were poison to the mind. They made you weak.

Never again.

CHAPTER SEVENTEEN

When Brutus woke, the plane had already touched down at the Uchben base outside Sedona. He must've been exhausted from the past weeks' events, because all he remembered was closing his eyes and then, boom. They were here.

Also, he'd had something very strange happen. *A wet dream? Really?* It must be Fina's presence and the state of permanent arousal she provoked. He'd dreamed that Fina and Colel were fighting over his penis, and no matter how many times he told Colel he didn't want her, she kept trying to grab him anyway. *"Oh, Colel... It's just not going to happen,"* he said.

To which she replied, *"But I haven't released you yet."*

"Only Fina can do that! Stop touching me."

It was a very strange dream, and when he woke, he had a little stain on his pants. *I wonder how it got on the outside.* Luckily, he was wearing camo, so no one would notice. *I bet Fina will find it very amusing, though.*

He smiled and looked around the cargo area with the huge open hatch in the back. Most of the women were outside standing on the tarmac, gathered around Cimil, who was giving directions to the prison and introducing them to one of the guards. The women appeared to be clawing at the poor man like a piece of meat, but that particular immortal was Andrus, an ex-assassin. He was mated to a half-succubus named Sadie and was only filling in to help out.

"Stop touching my pecs. That tickles," Andrus said, angry giggling.

Brutus would be laughing and going over to fuck with Andrus, but Fina was nowhere to be found. Brutus checked the bathroom, the cockpit, and the immediate surroundings.

Brutus left the hold. It was a beautiful morning with blue skies for miles. Just perfect to romance his warrior princess. "Hey, Cimil. Have you seen Fina?"

"Oh, yeah. She was the first to get off." Cimil looked down at his pants. "Make that the second. I think I saw her head into the prison with a pack of randy she-warriors out for a good shag."

"Fina? Are you sure?" he asked.

Cimil nodded. "Yeah. They were all screaming about getting some wood."

That's odd. Why wouldn't Fina wait for him? They were supposed to get married and then have their romantic event back at his place. He honestly couldn't wait to be alone with her.

"Thank you. If you see her, let her know I'm looking for her."

Cimil gave him a look that made his blood run cold.

"What?" he asked.

"Nothing…" She smiled sadistically.

"Cimil," he said sternly, "I have always been a loyal servant in your army. I have never interfered with your schemes and head trips, but if you know something, I beg you to tell me. If what you say is true, and we only have a few hours left, I deserve to spend them with the woman who changed my life."

"Oh…Bootius Maximus." She shook her head and tsked. "You know, they don't make 'em like you anymore—young, dumb, and hung—minus the young and dumb."

Huh?

She went on. "I am sorry to inform you that the happy ending—aka, giant cum-dump fest—you were planning for this evening just ain't gonna happen."

He frowned in confusion. "First of all, I planned to make love to her tonight, not dump my cum on her, in her, or anywhere in her proximity. Second, I find your choice of words to be offensive. Third, why won't it happen?"

Cimil chuckled and then stopped, bent over and moaned. "Oh! Oh! It's happening!"

"Now? You're giving birth now?" he asked.

"Call Roberto for me, wuddja?" She unzipped one of the tent pockets and produced a cell phone.

He hated to do this to a pregnant woman, but

Cimil was truly a rotten red apple. "Not until you tell me what's wrong with Fina."

Cimil moaned. "Three!"

"Three? I don't understand. What does that mean?"

Cimil winced. "The number of seconds until Minky arrives… Oh gods! Oh gods."

He didn't understand.

"One, two…"

Boom! The sky opened up as if someone had sliced through it with a giant knife, exposing the stars and darkness beyond the sun's reach.

Brutus, Andrus, and some of the warrior women still lurking around fell back. Cimil fell forward on her hands and knees.

Brutus blinked, trying to register the enormous blurry figure with fire for eyes shooting toward them like an asteroid. *Dear gods!* The flames licked around Minky's body, allowing him to see the shape and very recognizable horn. *What is wrong with her?*

At first he thought the creature had come to help Cimil, but no. It headed straight for an empty spot on the tarmac. Whatever the target, a ball of fire burst into the air and began swirling like a fiery tornado.

What in the world? He'd never seen anything like it.

"Brutus!" Cimil groaned. "Call Roberto!"

He got to his feet and helped Cimil up, which wasn't easy considering the situation and the ten-man tent she wore.

"What is that thing? What is happening?" he asked.

"Just Minky finding her mate, ending the plague." She groaned. "Who cares…Aah! They're coming out."

Brutus's head was spinning. "Are you being serious right now? The plague is over?"

"Yes! Yes!" Cimil barked, wincing and holding her hands over her enormous stomach. "The whole thing was because Minky was sangry!"

"Sangry?"

"Yeah!" Cimil screamed. "It's like hangry, but for sex!"

"Get the hell out." Why hadn't Cimil said so? Then again, who was he kidding? Cimil never said anything. She called it "spoiling the surprise." Also, she really lived for these moments when utter chaos suddenly resolved itself in the blink of an eye under the guise of fate. In other words, she justified her lies with the excuse of: It couldn't have worked out for the best had I told you all what was happening.

"It's really over? Everything's back to normal?" he asked.

Cimil shoved her phone at him, pregnant rage shooting from her eyes.

"Fine. I'll call." He grabbed it and started looking for the number. "I don't see Roberto."

"It's under Mummy Knob."

"Ah." He found the name and dialed.

Roberto picked up immediately. "Sugar cunt? That you?"

What a terrible name to call one's mate. Surprisingly, though, it sort of fit. "It's Brutus. I'm here on the tarmac in Sedona. Your wife is in labor."

"Oh. Be right there! Tell her to hang on!"

Brutus ended the call, and in an instant, Roberto appeared, grabbed Cimil, and then disappeared.

Meanwhile, the hissing and screeching continued from the tornado of fire on the landing strip.

Brutus shook his head. He had no clue what was going on. (A) Roberto had just sifted, something vampires had not been able to do for years—a long story. (B) Cimil had casually mentioned the plague was over because of…Minky's sex anger?

Maybe Cimil was lying again. Maybe she wasn't. *Only one way to find out.* Go to the prison and see if the quarantined immortals were back to normal. Hopefully, he'd find Fina there and figure out what was happening with them. He honestly didn't know what he'd done wrong.

He glanced over his shoulder at the twister of flames that showed no signs of letting up.

I really need to get a new job. This one was just getting too weird.

Fina figured that if she and Brutus weren't going to work out, then there was no reason to deprive herself of the pleasures of the flesh. She'd remained pure for centuries out of loyalty and tradition, only to discover their belief system was a hoax, a practical joke instigated by Cimil. At least they were all free now. No more holding back. No more self-sacrifice for false dogmas.

Perhaps I, too, will find a mate here in the immortal prison, a male truly worthy of me. Brutus wasn't who she thought, and she only had herself to blame. Her hot-and-bothered vagina had blinded her. *Sometimes, I only think with my little button.*

Well, now she was thinking with her big button. The one she could push and make shit happen.

The women found the prison entrance exactly where that fine, fine soldier named Andrus had told them it would be. Too bad he wasn't single, because a tall, muscular man like that looked like he knew how to please a woman. The only thing that turned her off was how much he looked like Brutus—the turquoise eyes, dark hair, and strong body.

Whatever. All that mattered now was that whichever male she chose from this prison of quarantined singles had a cock and knew how to use it.

The women accompanying her cheered as the elevator descended. What made her nervous was how all of the security controls had been disabled and someone had spray-painted *Do not enter! Danger! Turn back now!* on the wall and signed it "– Z."

I wonder who Z is…

The elevator stopped, and the shiny stainless steel doors slid open.

Fina and the eleven other women blinked, trying to digest what they saw. Everyone inside the nearly empty prison was quiet, sitting on the floor in the common area or in their unlocked jail cells. They were on laptops or phones. Their eyes were red and bleeding, not one of them moving.

"What do you think is happening?" said Jemma, one of the younger tribe members.

"I have no idea." Fina stepped out and passed through the open gate. Carefully, she tiptoed around the immortals—at least she assumed they were immortal. Fina looked over the shoulder of one man dressed in fatigues. *What in the world?* She leaned in a little.

Fina wasn't exactly sure what this was, so she checked two more immortals and returned to the women. "They appear to be on some program called Twitter and are writing mean messages about people—someone called the Orange Man and another they call Creepy Uncle."

"Oh. I heard about that. The humans call it trolling," said one of the women.

Whatever it was called, the infected prisoners seemed to be hypnotized by their activities, and these were not the evil, randy immortal men they'd hoped to find.

"It's a bust." Fina sighed, wondering where all

of the prisoners had gone. From what Brutus had said, it sounded like there were supposed to be a few thousand immortals imprisoned here.

She shrugged. *I guess no sex for me tonight.* The remaining males were glued to their electronics. "Gods, and I really wanted to get laid."

"Yeah, me too," said Jemma. "And I really hoped to find a husband, yanno? All these pregnancy hormones are making me crazy."

The other ten women agreed.

Fina frowned. "What do you mean, *pregnant?*"

"Yeah," Jemma explained. "Why do you think we all left the village? No way were we going to be knocked up and working like the queen demanded. Time to kick up our feet and be pampered a little, yanno?"

"But I-I don't understand. You're telling me you're *all* pregnant?" Fina winced, already knowing the truth. Her tribeswomen never minced words.

The eleven women nodded.

Well, I guess that whole thing about how and when we can conceive was a bunch of BS. Why was she surprised? Everything else they'd believed in turned out to be bogus.

"And the others who came with us on the plane?" Fina asked.

"All of us," Jemma confirmed. "We are all carrying Brutus's children."

Fina pressed her hands to her stomach. *I'm going to be sick.* "I can't believe this," she muttered. "All of them. With my man?"

"Whoa, whoa, whoa," Jemma interjected. "Ten minutes ago, when we got off the plane, you said you didn't want him anymore."

"Hey. I already called dibs," another sister barked.

Two more of Fina's tribeswomen spoke up, screaming about how they had a right to Brutus, too. Suddenly, all eleven were arguing over him.

The elevator doors opened, and out poured another twelve sisters. The first group told the second that the whole prison-inmate-sex-partner thing was a bust. Then the second group began staking claims on Brutus.

This isn't happening. Fina covered her face and groaned.

On the other hand, if they wanted to fight over Brutus, a man whose heart belonged to another, then who was she to stop them?

"Ladies!" Fina clapped her hands. "Since we are no longer bridled by Cimil's falsehoods, I evoke *the circle!*"

Her sisters gasped and then began cheering. No one had called upon the circle for centuries, because Cimil had banned it. Fortunately, that horrible goddess no longer called the shots. They were free to practice the old ways, the new ways, the sideways—anything they wanted.

"Come," Fina said. "Let us ask the hot man called Andrus where we might find lamp oil, lodging, and food."

CHAPTER EIGHTEEN

Brutus felt torn. He wanted to look for Fina, but he also needed to check on his dog and Señor Gato. Andrus said the kitten had returned on a separate plane and had been placed in Brutus's home after being passed along by Colel before her bees flipped. Andrus also reported that most of the prisoners had escaped and were down in the mall looting.

This is insanity! To top it all off, no one knew where the gods were, and that huge fireball outside continued spinning on the tarmac. Also, he saw zero signs of the plague ending. In fact, being here on base felt like he'd walked into a supernatural nightmare. He'd witnessed a group of were-creatures driving by in a Humvee. He'd seen vampires taking off in helicopters, going gods only knew where. He even saw some of the demigods, including one of his own men, loading up a truck with grenades—no doubt planning to terrorize some human cities.

I cannot even imagine what is happening downstairs in the mall. And there was absolutely nothing Brutus could do about any of it. He had no army, no telepathic platoon, no gods to assist.

He stood in the middle of the compound, where

several walkways intersected among cactus gardens and sculptures glorifying the gods, feeling like his head might explode.

"Hi, Brutus!"

He swiveled his head to spot his favorite dark-haired beauty in her black suede bikini. "Fina!" He'd never been so relieved.

He went in to hug her, but she stepped back and held out her hand to stop him.

"Don't. Touch. Me," she seethed.

He frowned. "What's the matter?"

She narrowed her eyes. "You know, I prepared an entire speech inside my head, starting with how my mother was right about men, to how it's people like you who make living in complete isolation in the jungle sound like heaven. But you know what? I have a feeling none of it will change what a miserable, lying asshole you are, so I'll simply leave it at... Hope one of my sisters makes you happy." Fina turned and started marching away toward the front of the compound.

"Fina. Hey! What in the world are you talking about?" He ran and cut her off.

"Stop it. I know you lied about wanting me."

"Is this because I refused to have sex with you? Is that what this is about?"

"No, it's about you still being in love with Colel and lying to me. What I don't get is why? Why pretend you didn't want her anymore, when you simply could've been honest and said you still loved her but might want to fuck me anyway? Why the romance and marriage proposal?"

"I honestly have no idea what you're talking about, Fina." He truly didn't.

She folded her arms, making her breasts push up in her little top. He tried not to notice, but it wasn't easy.

"So you have no feelings for her?" Fina seethed.

"Yes. I do, but they are feelings of loyalty and friendship. I will always care for her, but I want you."

"Then why did you call out for her when I was getting frisky with the General."

"When?" He frowned.

"Last night. On the plane." She wiggled her fingers at him.

"While I slept?" Brutus was starting to understand what had happened.

"Yes."

So that little sexy dream had been inspired by her hand. "Well, first of all, I feel a little violated. You could at least wake me up and get my consent. And second, you cannot hold a man accountable for his dreams."

"Dreams are a window into a person's soul and deepest desires."

"Well, last week I dreamed that I was trapped in Cimil's basement, and her unicorn was using my legs as chopsticks to eat giant grasshoppers. I seriously doubt that's on my bucket list in real life.

Besides, that dream with Colel wasn't sexual. At least, not the part with her in it. I was telling her to stop touching me."

Fina looked up at him and scratched her head behind her ear. She didn't look convinced.

"Fina, come on. If we are going to have a real relationship—" A sex fairy zoomed by in pursuit of a furry creature in a tiny red thong.

"What the hell was that?" Fina asked.

Brutus blinked. "I think it was Big Foot. Anyway, as I was saying, if we are going to have a relationship, one that will last forever and bring endless joy to each other's lives, then you need to start trusting me." He took her hand and pressed it to his rapidly thumping heart. "I want you, Fina. Truly and forever."

"You really mean it?" Her big dark eyes got glossy.

"Do you see me running off to find Colel when all hell is breaking loose?" he asked.

"No."

"That's right. And if Cimil is telling the truth this time, the plague might be ending, which means you and I will have eternity together. If she's wrong, then we have hours. Either way, I want to spend the rest of my life with you."

"Wait. Cimil said it was over?" She swiveled her head in both directions. "Sure the hell doesn't look like it."

"I don't know. Minky is spinning around with

something on the tarmac. Cimil said it was Minky's mate."

"What did the creature look like?" Fina asked.

"I have no idea. I think it's invisible."

"Mittens."

"What's a Mittens?" he asked.

"He's kind of like our village pet, but he's really a bloodthirsty creature that popped out of a lava-filled crevasse about two thousand years ago and sort of attached itself to us. He's invisible and ate anything that got within a mile of our village—he's how we've remained hidden from humans for so long. The Mittens name is to make him sound less scary to the children—not that we've had any in a long time."

Thank the gods I never came across him. "So you have no idea what Mittens is?"

"Not really. I've only seen him once when he took a mud bath. The locals down the river call him the Chupacabra. Some think he looks like a kra-ken—he loves water and eating boats. But I think he looks more like an enormous puppy with really big fangs and tentacles. He's kinda cute, though. That's why I changed his name from Fiery Hell-hound to Mittens."

Jesus. Brutus cringed. That thing was Minky's mate? He really hoped they didn't have offspring.

"Okay, well, whatever happens next, I suggest you and I get far away from here." Things were getting crazier by the second. "I know an ordained minister in town who also sells wonderful tacos. We can stop along the way to my place."

Fina smiled, and it warmed his heart.

"Brutus? I'm sorry about not trusting you."

"I understand. But there is no reason to doubt my intentions with you."

She bobbed her head. "Hey, listen, would you mind if we skipped the marriage thing? It's not a custom of my people, and I really just want to be with—"

An arrow whizzed by their heads.

"You get away from him!" a woman screamed from one of the rooftops.

"Let's get out of here." He reached for Fina's hand, but she stepped away.

"Sonofabitch." Fina threw her head back.

"What's wrong now?"

"I evoked the circle," she groaned her words.

"What's that?"

Fina shook her head. "Do you remember that Mad Max movie, the one with Tina Turner?"

"Uh, yeah. I'm a warrior who's fought off the apocalypse a thousand times. I own the whole Mad Max collection. Why?"

"Well, do you remember the Thunderdome?"

"Yes…?" He was beginning to sense this was not going to be good news.

"The circle is like that, but it's not a cage. It's made of fire, and it's how we resolve disputes over property. Everyone wanting to stake a claim enters the ring and fights until only one woman remains standing. In this case, it's ninety-three women. Ninety-four if you count me, too."

"What's the dispute?" Brutus asked, knowing he was not about to let Fina fight anyone for any reason. They needed to get the hell out of here while this whole plague apocalypse played out.

"You. You're the dispute," she replied, making a sign at the woman on the rooftop to back off.

"Me? I have no quarrel with anyone."

Fina scrubbed her face with her hands. "I surrendered my claim on you, and since all of the men in this compound are completely bonkers, my sisters all want a shot at having you."

"Why?" Because he certainly didn't want *them.*

"Because all ninety-three of my sisters who were on the plane are pregnant. With your babies."

Brutus blinked. "Very funny."

"I'm not joking. They are with child."

"No." Brutus felt his stomach knot and fall into his combat boots. Even his testicles shriveled in terror. How was this possible? Yes, yes. He knew how babies were made, but how had he gotten so many pregnant? "There must be some mistake. It's statistically impossible to impregnate so many women at the same time."

"Not when you're talking about a village of females who all cycle together and ovulated at the exact same time." Fina patted his arm. "And you nailed that window, baby. Congrats. We really needed new blood in the family."

It was great that Fina didn't seem to mind, but he sure the hell did! Having children with the woman you love was sacred. It was the one thing a couple did that connected them forever.

"What am I going to do?" This was terrible. And it wasn't as if he'd wanted to sleep with them. He only did it to be nice. Also, the second woman he'd had sex with—he couldn't recall her name since they all looked the same—tall, blonde, muscular and mean—told him they couldn't actually get pregnant like that. Some weird long explanation about birthdays and full moons and such.

"I don't know what *you're* going to do, but I know what I'm going to do," Fina said.

"Please tell me we are going to run far away and find a cave to hide in until this is all over?" If one more bizarre thing happened, he'd lose his fucking mind. He was a soldier, well-trained and disciplined. He was about structure and plans and winning battles. This situation was utter chaos. He controlled nothing. *Like a damned twig floating down a river during a rainstorm.*

"Brutus, I can't run. My honor is at stake."

"Meaning?" he asked.

"I'm going to have to enter the circle tonight and fight for you."

What the fuck? "No. I will not have it! I will not allow you and your sisters to fight to the death. It's out of the question." He had to put his foot down.

"Don't be ridiculous. We might be outside my village, but I'm still a leader. I wouldn't allow my pregnant sisters to kill each other when they're carrying the future of our tribe."

"Oh. Well, that's good to hear." He sighed with relief.

"We'll just kick the crap out of each other until no one can move. But don't worry. We're all very strong. And the fighting will make strong babies."

Errr... He knew nothing about babies. Forget about those born to immortal women. "No, Fina. I do not like this. It is unsafe, and if you haven't noticed, there is a bit of an issue we are dealing with. A WWE match in the middle of it all is not a wise idea. Call off the fight."

Fina's little lips puckered with frustration. "You don't think I can win, do you?"

Brutus puffed out his chest, trying to ignore the gang of were-penguins strolling by with cleavers. *Guess they found the cutlery shop in the mall.* "It's not about you winning, Fina. It is about the world falling apart around us. You, your sisters, our furbabies—we should all *leave*."

She shook her head. "We do not run from danger, and you of all people should respect that."

Yes, but now he had something to lose. He had *everything* to lose. And if the plague was ending, then maybe Cimil was lying about the end of the world. Then again, she'd sounded so sincere about both. *Fine.* He didn't know what was going to happen, and it fucking pissed him off. He was not a helpless man, but clearly in this situation, he was. If he could do one thing right, it would be to protect Fina and her sisters. *And my dog and kitty.* His home was only a few minutes from here, so hopefully the two animals were all right. Still, they all needed to get far away from civilization.

"Fine," he grumbled. "You're a warrior. So let's think this over strategically, as warriors. Let's say on the off chance you lose tonight, then what? Because I'm assuming you are bound by honor to let the victor have me. Are you going to allow that? And what happens to your precious honor when I refuse to be with the winner?" He couldn't believe he was arguing against his own code of honor, but so be it. The world was on its head.

Fina huffed. "I guess…I guess…I would have to honor the victor."

Dammit. "You missed the part where I said I will not go along with this. I am not some piece of property that can be traded or won in a competition."

"But you are. Well, at least in our culture."

He shook a finger at her. "That's—that's just wrong."

She shrugged. "You'd also be expected to cook and clean and stay home to care for your children— at least according to the old ways, before men were banned because of Cimil."

"I happen to be okay with that—I am a very secure male. But not the ownership part!" He yelled, feeling more than a little offended. "Let us speak with your sisters. We need to clear this all up and get the circle canceled."

"No." She stepped away. "And, technically, I'm not supposed to be talking to you before the match. It's considered bad manners since your ownership is being contested."

What am I? A damned goat! Brutus lifted a brow. He had to come up with something to call off this ridiculous ritual. No stupid circle was going to decide whom he spent his life with. Especially when the world might end in a few hours.

"I'll see you tonight by that big deity fountain in front of the compound." Fina started walking away.

"Where are you going?" he barked, feeling more frustrated than ever.

"To find food. I'll need my energy."

"But it is unsafe here. You must all leave!" he yelled.

"I'm an immortal warrior of the Great Waterfall of Manacapuru. I fear nothing!" She waved him off, and he felt his pants grow tighter.

Dammit. Why did she have to be so defiant? It was incredibly *hot!* He especially loved her fearless nature and brave heart. But this was a huge cluster of a situation, and he was not about to lose her to some tradition that had nothing to do with him.

Tradition. Rules. Didn't they have a library here in the compound? Perhaps he could find some information on their tribe. If not, he could always call and beg Cimil for a favor—she would know of some loophole or trick to get these women to call off the fight.

As he turned and started walking toward the garage, where he hoped he'd find at least a motorcycle or something with wheels, reality sank in. Hard.

I'm going to be a father. Of ninety-three children?

This world is truly going mad.

CHAPTER NINETEEN

Zac had thought he'd escaped the underground section of the prison without being noticed, but apparently he'd been wrong. The moment he exited the elevator and went to lock it down so there was no way in or out, those three flipped sex fairies jumped him. Then one of the creatures hit him with something, and the next thing he knew, he was waking up in the bondage store down in the mall, handcuffed to a steel display table meant for immortal S&M.

I knew selling immortal-strength handcuffs to the public was a mistake. But does anyone ever listen to me? No. I swear, I can't even... The ridiculousness of the situation was too much.

What he wouldn't give for it all to be over so that he and Tula could return to a normal, respectable immortal life filled with your basic paranormal creatures, such as gods, demigods, and vampires. He'd even be happy with the Maaskab still lurking in the shadows, biding their time to capture the gods. *Ah, the good old days. When apocalypses were simple.* And music made sense, consisting of one single drum. Perhaps a tambourine and some yodeling.

"Listen, ladies," he said to his captors, who were busy fondling his toes, "you can ask Minky if you want, but I'm not giving it up, okay? I am a one-woman god, and nothing you can say or do will change that." The sex fairies with their little pink and purple wings completely ignored him and pulled out a box from one of the cabinets.

"Feathers?" He cocked a brow. He hated to be tickled. Like, seriously.

"Hey! You guys get out of here!" Tula popped into the room, and the fairies flew off.

"Tula? I told you to stay away." He didn't want to risk her growing weak and disappearing forever.

"Yeah, well, all hell is breaking loose, and I'm not about to allow my man to be accosted by yet another horny creature. I mean, really. Who do they think they are?"

"I am the God of Temptation, my love. Do not be too hard on them. They can't help themselves."

"Ask me if I care."

"Is that a rhetorical question?" he questioned.

"Yes."

"I knew that."

"Uh-huh. So how am I going to get you out of here this time?" She looked around the room, which was covered in floor-to-ceiling bondage gear. Whips, chains, and more leather than even a badass god like himself knew what to do with.

"I don't see any two-ton magical doodies like we

had in Minky's cave," Tula said.

"No. They have only small unicorn turds over in the fetish section."

Tula shook her head. "I swear, Zac. I…"

Her voice faded. Though she was a disembodied spirit, her sorrow and frustration filled the entire room. "It just never ends! I try and I push and I hope and I trust, and all I get is kicked down over and over again. I can't take it anymore, Zac! I can't keep kidding myself that our love story was meant to be!" Salty ghost tears streamed down her pale ghostly face.

"Honey. Baby," he said softly. "Don't say that. The Universe is listening, and you don't want to upset her."

"No!" Tula shook her finger. "Fuck her. Fuck that stupid mean bitch!"

"Tula!" She never swore or thought mean things. It wasn't in her nature, but he also knew everyone had his or her limit. Tula had just reached hers.

"What?" Tula threw her hands to her sides. "Am I not allowed to say what's in my heart? Am I not allowed to be angry or feel betrayed? Does calling bullshit and yelling when I've been served a giant heaping helping of injustice make me a bad person?"

"No, sweetheart. It does not. And it's only natural to feel angry and frustrated by what seems like an impossible situation. But your energy is dimming. You only have so much to give. Why waste it? Why spend it on screaming when that won't solve the problem or make the Universe change?"

"So what the fuck do you propose I do, Zac? Huh? You want me to sit here and hope the world will throw us a bone?"

"Not at all, Tula. I'm merely asking you to focus on what really matters. Our love."

"Love. You think love is going to fix this giant cluster of fucks?" She huffed.

He couldn't believe he was seeing this side of Tula—the one who usually acted with her golden heart, who always saw the good in everyone. She never raised her voice or her hand, but she was always the first to extend it.

She is afraid. "It's the fear talking, my love. But let me assure you of *two* things: One, the world will never be perfect because *we* are not perfect. So stop getting upset over the things you cannot change. Focus your energy on the things within your control."

"I hate your stupid speech right now, so you'd better make number two really good."

"It is good. I love you. Nothing evil, unjust, beautiful, wonderful, or tragic can take that away. Our love has made this world a better place, and though you might not see it in this very moment of deep torment, I assure you that the tiny ripples created by our two hearts matter. Love always matters. It is the only thing that matters."

She frowned. "Yep. Just like I thought. I hated

number two. I don't want stupid mantras and life lessons of the great God of Temptation. I just want to be happy before I die. Before my time is up!"

"Then be happy. No one is stopping you," he pointed out. "Least of all me."

He watched as the lightbulb came on in Tula's transparent head. They had now, this moment, and she could either let that be enough and see the beauty in it, or she could stomp her feet because it wasn't perfect.

"I want to be happy. I do. But I'm nothing but a stupid ghost, powerless, without a body, and I want to touch you!"

"You're not stupid to me. To me, you're everything. So do you want to matter to a world who doesn't see you? Or do you want to matter to the one person who sees just how perfect you are?"

She swiped a tear from her eye, locking eyes with him. "I wish I could kiss you right now."

"Me, too." He toggled his head. "I could also go for some touching and sexing, but if I only get to stare at your face and those big blue eyes, I'll take it."

She bowed her head and pretended to press her mouth to his.

Wait. A second. Hold on. What the fuck?

Tula snapped her head back. "Ohmygod." She pressed her fingertips to her mouth. "I felt that."

Zac blinked, his heart thumping away with excitement. "Me, too!"

"You did?" she chirped.

"Yes! I did. Do it again!" he commanded.

Tula pressed her little lips to his, and he felt her sweet warmth. He felt it! Dear gods, their prayers had finally been answered.

She pulled away, her lower lip quivering. "What's happening right now?" she whispered.

"Woman, I do not know, but take off your fucking clothes this instant, including those ginormous panties, and get on top of me."

"Oh, gods. Oh, gods! This is happening!" With shaking hands, she whipped off her dress.

"Hurry!"

"This isn't how I imagined it, but I'll take what I can get!" She shimmied down his leather pants, exposing his thick hard manhood. "Wow. I haven't seen that in a while."

He had shown it to her a few times when they'd been experimenting with ghost sexing. It never panned out.

She hopped onto the table, straddled him, and leaned over, kissing him with so much force that it hurt. *I love it!* He would never complain about feeling her body on him, in him, around him, whatever! He'd take her any way he could get her!

Tula pulled back and beamed down at him. "I love you, Mr. Zac."

"I love you, too, Tula. But do me a favor; take it slow. In case this is our one and only time together, I want to remember every moment."

⮞ ⮜

One minute later…

"That was amazing, Tula." Zac threw back his head, floating on cloud nine. He'd never been ridden by a virgin like that, but it was an erotic experience he wouldn't soon forget.

"Seriously, Zac?" Tula growled, still straddling him. "I barely got a tingle! I mean, I waited years for that ending?"

He smirked. "Tula, I'm not a human male. I am a god. I can go as many times as you like—for days if you wish."

"Really?" She smiled.

"I can even come on demand. It's a gift." He gave her a little sample.

"Oh! Oh! Oh… Mr. Zac, I do believe you're forgiven."

The sheer fact that a tiny drop of his seed could excite her so, reinforced everything he felt so deeply in his heart. "I love you, woman. I love you so much. Think you can find a key around here somewhere?" He jerked his wrists, wanting to touch her smooth, *solid* skin.

"I probably could, Mr. Zac, but my sweet innocent days are over. I've got some dirty fantasies now, and most of them involve you being at my mercy."

Not going to complain. "The God of Temptation approves. Especially because nothing could tempt me to deny you an ounce of happiness after everything you've been through."

"Can we have a big wedding?" She clapped.

"Done."

"A summer villa in Greece?" she asked.

"Done."

"A charity to help children afflicted by apocalyptic events?" Her blue eyes lit up.

"Absolutely," he replied.

Her joyful smile melted away. "But what if I fade in an hour? What if this was just a consolation prize from the Universe?"

He offered her his warmest, sincerest grin. "Then we are just like every other couple in the world, forced to live in the moment, who cannot allow themselves to forget how precious their love is."

"I like that." She sighed contentedly.

"Kiss me again and take your pleasure. I give you one hour and then it's my turn." He also had some fantasies. And none of them involved being in a mall while strange creatures watched through the plate-glass window.

CHAPTER TWENTY

Bent with worry, Brutus went to check that his dog and kitten were in fact safe and sound at his house just outside town. But on the way there and back to the compound, he'd nearly lost his head five different times. The immortal chaos was spilling over into the mortal world—car accidents, looting pastry shops, people spray-painting buildings with colorful images of bloodthirsty unicorns. Some guy in a clown suit was literally taking dumps on people's cars. While they were driving. Brutus had never seen anything like it! Had he woken up on another planet? Worse yet, the craziness made him late!

It was a few minutes until the circle began, and he had no idea what to do.

The gods were missing.

His men had flipped.

The prisoners were no longer quarantined.

The Uchben library had nothing on Fina's people.

Cimil wasn't answering her phone.

His inner warrior screamed for him to act and do whatever it took to get Fina away since she refused to back down from this circle crap.

Showered, wearing clean black fatigues, and armed to the teeth with his favorite sword and two different sidearms, Brutus approached the fountain in front of the compound.

"Meow!"

"Woof!"

Brutus glanced down at the two furry faces protruding from the pet pack strapped to his chest. He *had* found both animals deposited in his home with a note from one of his men apologizing for flipping. *So like them. Always thinking of the team first.* Even when they turned evil, his men showed respect. Maybe respect wasn't something that changed with the tides. Good or bad, respect could be shown by the best or worst.

"All will be well, my friends." Brutus patted his furkids' soft heads and gazed out across the darkening horizon. Something deep inside his immortal bones quaked. His skin tightened; his muscles tensed; his asshole puckered. Whatever was about to go down, he sensed it was something big.

Also, was it his imagination, or had the Minky-Mittens fireball grown bigger since he'd left? The tarmac was down the hill a ways, but the flames looked like they were twenty stories high. Whatever Minky and Mittens were doing, it had to be intense.

Brutus made his way to the front of the compound overlooking miles of open desert. As he approached the fountain of the gods, which had tiny statues of…you guessed it, the gods, he spotted Fina. She sat at the edge of a large flaming circle, alongside the other women. They had their eyes closed and legs crossed. Several hundred flipped immortal spectators—escapees from the prison—cheered for blood and were drinking beer. Brutus even spotted Ah-Ciliz and K'ak, foaming at the mouth. *Well, at least Akna isn't here.* The Goddess of Fertility could make anything multiply, including rage.

He went up behind Fina and was about to beg her to cease this ridiculousness, but his watch beeped, indicating it was eight o'clock.

The women's dark eyes sprang open. They stood and stepped through the fire into the circle.

The men around them howled.

"Stop it! Have you no respect for the mothers of my children?" Seriously. It was gross. Brutus called out to Fina, "Babe! I really don't see the point in you doing this. I will not allow a silly competition to determine who I spend my life with. And I refuse to spend one more day without you."

She didn't listen, of course.

Fina took her position at the center of the ring. "To the end. Only one will leave. The prize for the victor."

Before he could conjure a thought, the women began swinging, punching, and fighting. He clenched his fists as one of the women landed a blow on Fina's temple, and she flew back.

Godsdammit! It was not in his nature to sit by while a battle was fought, and he sure as hell wasn't going to allow his woman to be slugged in the face.

The women kept swinging and clawing. Suddenly, one of them whipped out a knife. Then another.

Oh crap! This was no longer a friendly boxing match. Then he noticed that the women's eyes had turned into dark orbs.

They were flipping! But of course they were! It had only been a matter of time.

"Fina! Get out of there!" Brutus yelled.

But she wasn't listening. None of them were.

"Here. Hold my kitten and dog, wuddja?" Brutus turned to the guy next to him but noticed the man also had two pits of black for eyes. "Never mind." Brutus's eyes scanned the crowd. V*ampire. Vampire. Were-hippo? Demigod, demon, sex fairy. Dammit.* Everyone was evil to the core, and he needed someone to hold his critters.

Ah. Maaskab! He darted over and shoved the pet pack at the Mayan priest, whose entire body was caked in dry blood. His long black hair was dreaded with mud and adorned with human teeth.

"Hey, buddy. Mind helping me out and holding my pets for a minute?" Brutus asked.

"*Yaan in jantik a nej peek' yáax.*"

"Cool. Thanks." Brutus handed over his pack and then turned his attention toward the ring. "All right, ladies. Make some room."

Brutus jumped in the circle and pulled out his sword, running straight for Fina to guard her back, but he instantly realized he had two major problems. One, he couldn't stab a pregnant woman carrying his child. Two, these women had no qualms about stabbing him.

Sonofbi—he sidestepped as one of the ladies jabbed straight for his stomach. Then a fist flew toward him, and he ducked and pushed. The woman stumbled out of the circle.

"Hey! That's cheating," she griped.

Cheating? He called that saving his ass.

He noticed that she tried to reenter the circle but couldn't. Was this some sort of supernatural sumo match? If you stepped out of the ring, you forfeited?

Hmmm... He grabbed one of the unarmed women from behind, lifted her, and carried her out.

"You sonofabitch!" she yelled, and like the first woman, she couldn't reenter.

This was it. The solution!

Brutus began pushing, carrying, and dragging them out of the ring. The few with knives were the toughest.

"I'm going to kill you!" He heard Fina yell, and she dove for one of her sisters who had a knife. The woman stumbled out of the ring and began fighting with one of the infected soldiers. *And it's one of mine.* Not good. They were extremely efficient killing machines.

Brutus froze. That woman, no matter how evil at the moment, was still pregnant.

His head whipped back and forth, noting more of the women on the outside of the ring attacking vampires and some of the other male onlookers. *Jesus.*

He looked back at Fina, who was now in a headlock and turning blue.

He ran over and tried to pull the woman off, but she refused to relinquish her grip.

He could kill the woman, but how could he live with himself?

Brutus pulled again and wrapped his arm around the woman's neck. He hoped she'd simply pass out.

Just as he felt her stop struggling and drop Fina, there was a sharp pain in his side. He glanced down to find a dagger sticking into him.

Brutus fell to the ground, the pain shooting through him. Suddenly, Fina was on him. Straddling his torso. She jerked the dagger from his side and raised it above his head.

All he could do was stare into her dark empty eyes and pray there was some piece of her still inside, fighting this evil.

"Fina…don't. Just drop the knife. This isn't you. You're not in control."

She paused for a second.

Suddenly, the fireball that had been spinning for hours on the tarmac shot high into the sky. Everyone stilled, hypnotized by the bright white light.

What is that?

The light began shrinking to almost nothing and then…

Boom! It exploded.

CHAPTER TWENTY-ONE

Tula looked over at Zac, who was still handcuffed to the steel table. She sighed with the deepest contentment known to man. Or woman. "Mr. Zac, that was amazing."

"It was. It truly was. You were also very good."

She laughed and swatted his bare chest. "Very funny. Just for that, I think I'll leave you here for a few more hours."

"As long as you keep having sex with me."

She had to admit, having her body back felt amazing. She felt her stomach rumble, her heart beating, and the air entering her lungs. She never imagined that such simple things, things she used to take for granted, would feel so...so...wonderful! But hands down, having real actual sex with Zac had been better than she imagined. At first it was a little uncomfortable, due to his deific size, but once they got going, she knew he hadn't been exaggerating. He *was* a magnificent lover. And yes, he truly could go and go and go!

"Zac?" She snuggled her cheek into his chiseled bare chest.

"Yes?"

"What happens next?" she asked.

"I don't actually know. To be honest, I have been so focused on getting you into your body and for us to have this moment, that nothing else really mattered."

"Do you think Minky will come after you?"

"Who knows? But if she does, then she'd better like watching."

"What do you think happened?" she asked. "I mean, I got my body back, so…"

Zac turned his head, piercing her with his stunning turquoise eyes. "Tula, if you don't mind, I would really like to just enjoy this moment."

He was right. They'd both been through so much, and if she'd learned anything through it all, it was that you had to savor the truly magical moments. You just never knew when the Universe would veer left and turn your life on its head. "Whatever happens next, Zac, I want you to know that I will always love you. In this plane or any plane of existence. In this life or the next. My soul is bound to yours forever."

Zac blinked at her and smiled. The way his eyes sparkled with the deepest love made her heart weep with joy. "Thank you, Tula. I feel the same. And if it weren't for you, I never would have become the awesome, generous god that I am. I have you to thank for everything wonderful in my life and for making me whole."

Those were just about the sweetest words she

could ever hope to hear from any man.

"Wow! I need to use the little girls' room. Isn't that awesome?" She never thought she'd be so excited to tinkle.

"They probably have a bathroom back there." He jerked his head toward the back storeroom.

"Okay. Be right back." She hopped off the table, enjoying the feel of gravity holding her feet to the floor.

"Hurry up. I need you to find the keys so we can get out of here. Gods know what other crazy shit is going to happen today."

She went through the door leading to the storeroom. "Oh. There's a bathroom!" She did her business and then washed her hands. "Hey. What if we go and check on my parents? They've been really worried about—" Tula walked out of the store's bathroom only to find an empty table. The handcuffs were simply dangling. "Zac?" She looked around the small boutique and then went out front. There was no sign of him anywhere. And the mall was empty.

A weird energy and loud humming in the air told her something was very wrong.

❧ ❦

Emma watched her beautiful husband, Votan, the God of Death and War, with his shiny blue-black mane, climb the large tree extending over the calm waters of Lake Bacalar. It was his and their kids' favorite thing to do. They'd spent the entire day scaling it and then jumping into the warm bath-like water.

At the moment, the children were inside the villa, eating a late supper with the nanny. The two of them had decided to stay and have a little alone time. After all, it was a beautiful night, and Emma was enjoying all of the memories of her first trip here to the lake. She'd never forget how scared she'd felt getting on the plane in New York City to come all the way down here to Mexico, near the border of Belize, all because a male voice in her head told her to do it. Little had she known that the voice belonged to a deity, the man who would be her forever love. But the moment she laid eyes on him, her heart knew.

Emma let her legs dangle off the dock while Guy, her nickname for Votan, climbed to the edge of the thick branch. She loved how he was seventy thousand years old but still loved to play. He also loved his cars. The faster, the more expensive, the better.

She felt a little pinch on her ankle. "Ow." She pulled her leg from the water and itched the spot. *Dang mosquitos.*

When she looked back up at the tree, Guy was gone.

"Guy?" She stood up and peered into the dark water. "Guy!" But there was no sign of him anywhere. She ran inside and got a flashlight, but she already knew. She could feel it in her gut and deep in her soul. The connection, their mate's bond, was gone.

Ohmygod... What just happened?

êê êê

Roberto was so excited to finally meet his five new offspring. He cared not if they were tiny bloodsucking demons or, worse, if they ended up being nice ordinary people. After everything he and Cimil had gone through—apocalypses, her going to merman jail, him not believing she was pregnant, and the plague—the only thing that mattered now was that they were together. Here in their Hollywood hills home.

With a cup of ice chips in hand, he sifted back to their bedroom. He had no clue why or how he'd suddenly been able to use his gift of teleportation again, but it had certainly come in handy.

"Honey, I brought you some..." He looked around the all-hot-pink room, but Cimil was nowhere to be found. "Cimil! Cimil!" Five newborn redheaded baby girls lay on the bed, blinking up at him.

Dear gods. His wife was gone, but the children in her belly had been left behind.

êê êê

Fina felt like her skin was on fire. The heat had started from the top of her head and worked its way down to the tips of her toes. Whatever was happening, she couldn't move.

"Fina!" Brutus hovered over her, his blue eyes shimmering with relief. "Thank the gods you're all right."

Suddenly, whatever had a hold of her let go. She heaved out a breath. "What happened?" She felt like she'd had the wind knocked out of her.

Brutus helped her sit up. All around them, others were lying on the ground, too, and waking up.

"I do not know," he said. "You were possessed one second, fighting in the circle, and then there was an explosion."

He brushed his large hand through her hair. "How do you feel?"

"Good. I guess. A little weak though." Her muscles felt softer and heavier. "But I think there's something wrong with my vision. Your eyes look powder blue." He normally had striking turquoise eyes, the telltale sign of the light of the gods coursing through his veins.

Brutus frowned and looked around at the few hundred people waking up. Several were groaning and rubbing their heads.

"I'm human again!" one of the vampires called out.

What the what? Fina looked up at Brutus. "What's going on?"

"I do not know, my love, but you are not the only one who feels strange." He helped her to her feet.

A small meow off in the distance rang out.

She and Brutus exchanged glances. "Señor Gato! Niccolo!" Brutus moved toward the sound, stepping over sleeping people.

A man with clean tanned skin, long black dreads, wearing a suede thong, had the two animals snuggled to his chest.

"There you are," Brutus said.

Fina crouched down to pick the kitten up, noting the human teeth in the man's hair. "Is that a Maaskab?"

"*Was* a Maaskab." Brutus picked up his dog. "He looks normal now."

"What is going on?" Fina asked just as Señor Gato scratched her arm. "Ouch!" Blood trickled out of the tiny gash. Normally she wouldn't react to a minor wound. "Brutus, I think we've all turned human. And look, everyone is calm and doesn't have that angry constipated expression."

Brutus raised a dark brow. "Then the plague is truly over, just as Cimil said, but I think it took all of our supernatural energy with it." He scratched the back of his head. "Because I feel mortal now, too."

CHAPTER TWENTY-TWO

Brutus wanted nothing more than to take Fina to his place, bend her over his kitchen counter, and pound his cock into her. Yes, he was romantic like that. And the wait to be with her felt like torture.

Unfortunately, something big had happened, and no one knew why or what to do. Was it the result of Minky and Mittens's exploding fireball of love? Was it the Universe's way of putting an end to a plague that was never meant to be, as he suspected?

Brutus didn't know, but reports from all over the world had started coming in to the base's command center: The vampires, demigods, and were-creatures were now human. Any full-blooded supernatural beings were simply gone. Poof! No more incubi. Poof! No more sex fairies.

"I have some disturbing news." Andrus, once a demigod, entered the command center stadium room, where every abled body, including Fina's sisters, was helping assess the situation by taking calls and gathering information. The chief, Gabrán, was in his office at the end of the hall, trying to contact the various Uchben bases and determine who might still be alive.

Andrus groaned and ran his hand through his dark hair. "Dammit. Would you look at this?" He held out his hand. Two black hairs were stuck to his finger. "I'm already going bald. Being mortal sucks. And did you know my half-incubus wife is now completely human?"

Brutus could think of worse things, to be honest. "I'm sure she's still the same lovely woman you fell for."

"Yeah, but she's not nearly as horny. She just told me she was too tired for sex in the janitor closet. Can you believe that?"

Brutus didn't have time for this. "Andrus," he growled, "what is your news?"

"Ah. Okay, so I was able to get a hold of most of the gods' mates—who are all on their way here to help, by the way—but they all said the exact same thing: The gods are missing. They disappeared about the same time Minky exploded."

Brutus couldn't believe this. "The gods are missing?" But how? But why?

"And so is anything supernatural, Brutus. Everyone who was once human is now human again. Even Roberto, Cimil's husband, says he's back to his old pharaoh self, and his kids are well-behaved."

Dear gods. This really was strange. But what could they do? There was no game plan, contingencies or history of such events to guide them.

Brutus felt an odd sensation wash over him. His

eyes were closing, and his stomach hurt like hell. He pushed his hand to his abs.

"I know, right?" Andrus said. "I can't make it stop either. I'm so hungry."

Brutus couldn't believe it, but he had to make the call. "Everyone! May I have your attention, please?"

The room of literal people stopped their activities and listened.

He continued, "It's been a very long and trying night, but I think everyone needs to call it a day. There are plenty of beds in the barracks. If you are hungry, there are sandwiches down in the food court." Thanks to some of Fina's people who'd volunteered to make coffee and snacks. "We will reconvene at eight a.m. No. Wait. Make that eleven. I think we could all use the extra sleep." Andrus was right! Being mortal sucked. He felt so…normal and human and tired.

Fina walked in, carrying a tray of coffee. "Where's everyone going?"

"To bed. And I suggest we do the same."

She smiled. "I thought you'd never ask."

"If I've learned one thing, it's that the disasters never stop coming. And now that we are human again, we really do need to sleep."

"Sleep?" She raised a dark brow. "That's the last thing I want."

❧ ❦

Brutus had felt the General stirring the entire drive home in the military truck he'd borrowed. The only thing stopping him from taking Fina on the side of the road en route to his house was the fact that Señor Gato and Niccolo were with them and needed to be fed.

Just as the sun was coming up, they hit the long dirt road leading to his house. The sun seemed so much brighter today—reds and flaming oranges setting the desert cliffs on fire. It was magnificent seeing the world with these new human eyes.

"Is it just me," he said, "or does everything feel different, more alive somehow?"

"I'm so glad it's not just me. I feel like I woke up on another planet, and this one is so much more colorful."

Brutus pulled up in front of his adobe. The home was a small one-bedroom with nopales and other cacti in the front yard—plants that didn't require watering during his long assignments. It was nothing fancy, but the land around it was his and peaceful. After so many years, it had become his sanctuary, a place where he could unwind. And knit.

"Are you ready?" Brutus shut off the engine, feeling his hands tremble. Never in his life had he been so nervous about being with a woman. His heart felt like it might jump out of his body. His cock was aching with need.

"Oh yeah…I'm ready." Fina flashed a huge smile and popped the door. He loved that she still wore her native clothing—basically nothing. He'd had all sorts of fantasies about removing her little suede bikini and finally getting a peek at what was underneath. "But I'm starving. How about a snack?"

He couldn't argue. Their new mortal bodies would require nourishment for this event.

"You feed the furkids. I'll make grilled cheese. Deal?" he said.

"Deal."

They both hopped from the truck, and he unlocked the front door with the keypad. "The house might be old, but it's a fortress." He pushed open the front door—a hand-carved piece of art that was five inches thick.

They stepped inside the cozy living room with Saltillo tile and a big overstuffed beige couch covered in a handmade quilt he'd done himself to keep the dog hair off the fabric.

"It's lovely," Fina said.

"Would you like a quick tour?" he asked, trying to be a gentleman.

"Later. Where's the food?"

"Kitchen's through there." He pointed to the arched doorway edged with hand-painted tiles embedded in the plaster. He'd made those himself, too. "There's some dry food in the pantry to the side of the fridge. You can open a can of tuna for Señor Gato." Fina had the animals fed in one minute flat. Brutus got to work with the frying pan on his big gas stove on the center island, and had their sandwiches done lickety-split. The cheddar slices didn't taste too wonderful, since they'd been in the freezer, but they both sat at the little breakfast table, near the window in the kitchen, and scarfed down their food.

"Brutus?" Fina looked up at him from her empty plate.

"Yes?" His heart started pounding in his chest again.

"I'm nervous."

"Me too," he admitted.

She raised one brow and gave him a strange look.

"Though, not for the same reason as you," he added. "It's just…I've never been with someone who—"

"Was a virgin?" she added.

"No. Well, yes. That's true, but I'm nervous because I want you so badly."

She grinned, making two little lines form on either side of her almond-shaped eyes. Those were new. He sort of loved them. *Look at us, already growing old together.*

"That's a good thing, right?" she said.

"Yes; however, there's a part of me that fears once we are together, it will change things between us."

She tilted her head to one side. "You think you won't want me afterward?"

"No. The opposite. I fear that once I have

you…" He wanted to say that he would never want to leave her, and that his job, especially now that the gods were missing, would take him away. Weeks, maybe months. The Uchben like himself wouldn't rest until the gods were found.

"What?" she prodded.

He didn't want to ruin the moment. "Nothing. I'll just be the happiest man on the planet. That's all."

"Well then." She rose from the table, flashed a big smile, and sauntered off, wiggling those hips for him. "You coming?" she called out from the bedroom.

No, but I will be in two seconds if I don't calm down.

He got a cold glass of water from the fridge and then turned, finding her standing naked in the doorway.

He nearly dropped his glass as he drank in her naked body. He'd never seen such a beautiful woman. The curve of her hips, the fullness of her breasts, the toned legs and arms. She was soft and firm and everything woman.

Brutus set down his glass on the counter, marched over, and cupped her face. "You have no idea how long I've waited for you."

"I thought we just met a few weeks ago."

He shook his head. "No, Fina. What I feel for you right now, I've been waiting to feel for hundreds of years."

He dipped his head and kissed her hard. It was strange having to be gentle. Well, more gentle than usual.

He scooped her up, his mouth never leaving hers. Her lips were sweeter than any fruit or candy he'd ever tasted. Her body was hotter than any fire. The feelings inside his human heart were more intense than any emotion he'd ever known. Was this what humans felt when they were with someone they loved? It was incredible!

The strange thing was, he'd been born human, but perhaps he'd been immortal for so long that he'd forgotten what it felt like to truly be alive. In the moment. Experiencing every sound, smell, and sensation.

The feelings from before, when life didn't seem to matter because he'd been there, done that, were gone. There was something terrifyingly wonderful about knowing his body would grow old and that life could no longer be taken for granted, that every moment together had to be cherished and savored.

Brutus suddenly felt a knowing in his chest, a comfort or fullness that had never been there before, as if the Universe herself had been by his side the entire time, watching over him, leading him to this exact moment. Of course, it was silly to believe he mattered to her—such an enormous complex creature that spent her days weaving endless webs of life—but how else could he explain the perfection of this moment? Of Fina? Of them? Had the plague not occurred, had his heart not been broken by Colel, he never would have gone to that jungle and sought out Fina's tribe.

Brutus carried Fina to the bed and laid her down. His woman. Naked. Beautiful. Smart. He pulled off his black tee and shed his dark camo pants while she watched with hungry eyes.

"I am going to make your first time so fucking good," he said, "you won't ever want to leave this bed."

He stretched out next to her, letting his fingertips roam over the soft skin of her stomach, up to her breast.

When he looked into her eyes, he saw...well, eyelids. Fina was passed out. Totally gone. Snoring.

"Fina?" he whispered, but she didn't move. He chuckled. *My princess is tired. And so beautiful.* He brushed back the hair from her face, noting the golden streak on her temple. She truly was gorgeous. So unique.

"I waited this long, I don't mind waiting some more." He placed a gentle kiss on her mouth. "Just know that I could never ask for a better woman to be human with. Never doubt that, Fina. Never."

CHAPTER TWENTY-THREE

When Fina woke later that morning, it was to a huge gorgeous naked warrior at her side and a loud knock on the front door. Señor Gato was going crazy meowing. Brutus's old dog, Niccolo, just lay there at the foot of the bed.

She got up from the bed, noting that her body was also naked but still just as tightly wound as the day before. And the day before that.

"Oh, great. I must've fallen asleep." So much for their big night of passionate mind-blowing sex.

She opened the small closet door in the corner of the bedroom and grabbed one of Brutus's long white dress shirts.

The knocking continued. "I'm coming. I'm coming."

She went to the front door and peeked out the little hatch thing in the center. It was her sister Chela, one of the oldest.

Fina opened the door and stepped outside so as not to wake Brutus. "Hi. What's going on?"

"We're leaving—going back to our village."

"What? Why?" Fina asked.

"We all gathered this morning to offer our

words of peace over the circle incident. And after much discussion, we all agreed that this is no place to raise our daughters. These modern people are nuts!"

Fina couldn't exactly argue. She'd lived in both worlds, spending summers in the jungle to bring back her knowledge to the others, and the rest of her time at school. This modern world was loud and chaotic. People were out of touch with nature. On the other hand, their access to knowledge and books was incredible. Anything you wanted to know or learn about was at the touch of a fingertip.

But what was the point of having so much information if humans ignored it or used it to manipulate each other for power?

"I understand." Fina bobbed her head.

"Good. I'm glad. We leave within the hour."

"So soon?"

"Yes," replied Chela. "One of the soldiers is flying a cargo plane to Argentina to pick up a group of wounded Uchben. Apparently, their doctor was a hydra and disappeared. Anyway, he said he should be able to land at the old base near our village and drop us off."

"Wow. Okay. Just give me a moment to find some other clothing." Fina wanted time to say goodbye to everyone. Who knew when she'd be able to see them again. Everything here was a mess, and Brutus was the only one who seemed to know what to do—how to organize the remaining soldiers and gather information so they might figure out what had happened with Minky and Mittens.

"What you have on is fine for the trip," Chela said. "I can cut it up and make you a new and proper outfit on the plane."

Fina frowned. "Plane? But I'm not going with you."

"Why not?"

Where to start? "My mother still wants to cook my head in a pot, and even if that weren't true, I refuse to live under tyranny and oppression."

Chela scoffed. "But you expect us to?"

"Well, if you're going back, you know what to expect." They weren't naïve children.

"Fina, your mother only had power because we granted it to her. Without our compliance, she is nothing. That's why you must come. We will need a new leader, a sister we trust and respect."

"But I…" Fina hadn't even considered going back. And now she had Brutus.

"Sister, we all heard you that morning, talking of change and a better life for all of us. We are behind you, but if we return without your leadership, I'm afraid that too many will fall into old patterns and bow to the queen and her followers."

Fina knew that Chela spoke the truth.

"Um, I just need to talk to Brutus. Either way, I'll see you at the tarmac."

Chela did not like that answer, and Fina couldn't blame her. The women wanted assurances that Fina would be going home with them.

"Sure. Fine. But just remember," she added, "if you come with us and take over, your man will be welcome, too." Chela marched to the beige-camo-painted Jeep in the driveway, where one of the Uchben soldiers was waiting behind the wheel. The guy kept poking at his incisors and looking in the vanity mirror.

Must be an ex-vampire. This adjustment to new human bodies would be difficult for everyone.

"Where will I be welcome?" Brutus's sexy gravelly voice echoed from the doorway of the bedroom, where he stood buck naked.

Oh wow. She felt her body instantly getting hotter, especially her face and chest. She wanted him so badly, it hurt to look at him. *Like being super hungry and staring at a giant cheeseburger.*

Dammit. Why can't I stop thinking about food?

"Um." She closed the front door. "That was one of my sisters, soon to be the mother of one of your ninety-three children. I have great news about that, by the way."

"Oh?" He folded his huge arms over his bare chest.

"Yeah. They're all returning to the village to raise the children somewhere safe."

"What about your mother?" he asked.

"That's part of the good news!" Fina was afraid to spit this out. What if he said no? "The women have all decided to fire Queen Chacacacakhan and put me in her place."

He scratched the inky stubble on his strong chin. Gods, she loved that chin. It was the type a girl could sit on.

"I don't see how that will work if you're so far away and..." His words faded off. "You're leaving, aren't you?"

"Brutus, I hoped that we would be leaving together. The plane departs in an hour, and you'll be welcome in my village if I'm in charge."

He frowned. "What makes you think I would ever return to that...that place? No. We are staying here, where we are needed."

Fina felt her heart splitting in two. "That place is my home. Those people are my family. They need me."

"I need you. And might I remind you that a few days ago, they were going to slit your throat, and then after that, they were chasing you through the jungle, determined to kill you." His voice boomed, filling the small room like a crack of thunder.

"That's only because my mother would have made them do it, and they were afraid of her."

Brutus turned and disappeared into his bedroom. By the time she caught up, he was already sliding on a pair of black leather pants.

Oh dear gods. He looks sexy. No. No. Focus. We are fighting about something very important. What was it? Oh yeah... "Brutus, look. If I don't go with them, then the chances of my mother instilling fear and controlling them again is fairly high. I have to go. I have to stand up to her and make sure she's thrown into the fiery pits of hell where she came from."

"You have a hellfire pit in your village?"

"No. That's just what we call it. It's more a deep crevasse with sludge at the bottom."

"Well, I wish your tribe luck throwing the queen into it, but *we* are staying here."

Why did he speak like he was in charge? "And what about your daughters? What about their futures?"

"I was merely a sperm donor, and you know that. I can't all of a sudden give up my responsibilities and turn my back on my men because you decided to tie me to a tree and let your sisters take advantage of me."

Ugh. Fina huffed. "You enjoyed it, and you know it."

"Yeah, and so did you. Don't think I didn't see you behind that tree, watching."

"So? I thought you were sexy and beautiful, and maybe I was jealous that I wasn't one of them."

He went to his dresser and pulled out a black T-shirt. "Well, isn't that funny, because here I am, willing to give you all of this," he swept his hand over his body as if presenting a prize, "and you're running away to be with the same people who betrayed you, tracked you like an animal, and wanted to kill you."

He was right. She knew it, too. "But they want change, Brutus. And I hold no ill will toward them. Otherwise, I wouldn't have gotten on a plane with them. They wouldn't have gotten on a plane with me."

"Then let them get back on it and leave!" he yelled. "And if you really want to go, too, then I'm not stopping you. But just know you are throwing away something very special."

Fina felt his words like a sword through the heart. Why wouldn't he even consider her proposal? "I think if you really wanted to be with me, you would at the very least try to find a way to compromise so that we both get what we want. But all I'm seeing is a stubborn male who wants to win. It's all or nothing. Your way or no way." She balled her fists. "I hate to say it, but my mother was right. Men are poison." And her heart agreed. "I'm so glad I didn't sleep with you!"

"Yeah, well…me, too," he threw back.

"Fine."

"Fine," he said and then marched into the living room. "And you're crazy if you think you're taking my cat."

"That's my cat!"

"Really?" Brutus set the kitten down on the Saltillo floor and stepped back. The little bastard walked right to him and rubbed its face on Brutus's ankle.

Brutus smiled like he'd won some great battle fit

for the history books.

"Whatever." Fina threw her hands in the air. "Keep the animal. I'll be too busy raising your children anyway."

Fina stomped outside, realizing she had no way of getting to the airstrip, which was probably fifteen miles away. She turned and shot Brutus a hard look.

"I'll give you a ride. I'm going to the base anyway." He grabbed his keys and shut the door.

They both got in the truck. She'd never seen Brutus angry—he'd always kept his cool like a well-trained soldier—but his jaw was pulsing, and with the grip he had on the steering wheel, she was pretty sure he was going to bend it or pull it from the dash.

She, on the other hand, felt hurt. She wanted him. She might even love him. No, she already did. She had to. Otherwise, she wouldn't feel like she'd just died on the inside.

"I would never do this to you," she grumbled as they pulled out of the driveway onto the main road into town.

"Do what? Ask me to leave behind my life, my people, my home? I think you did exactly that."

She turned to face him, noting his light blue eyes focused sharply on the road. "I only asked that you come with me. I never said you had to live there full time or stay and never leave."

"The world might end in a day, and I want to spend it with you."

"You don't honestly believe that it's all over?"

"Cimil said so."

"And Cimil lies like a doormat. She only has one setting, which is chaos. What she probably meant was that *she* was ending. Her time on earth is over!"

"Fine. You're probably right since I know she declares the end of the world five times a day. But that doesn't change the fact that you're leaving."

"Come with me!" she argued. It was so damned simple. Just get on the godsdamned plane!

"What kind of life would we have together, huh? I was already thinking about how difficult it would be to leave you for weeks at a time. Now you suggest we remain separated for months? Who will be here for me when I come home and I'm hungry or need my camo pants washed?"

Fina growled. "Wait. So you expected me to sit at home, waiting for you with the cat and dog, while you went out on missions?" What an archaic barbarian.

"I could think of worse things. Also, the base is just a few minutes' drive, and they always need people. Janitors. Gardeners—you're good with a broom and plants, right? It's not as though you wouldn't have things to do."

Wow. I made a huge mistake with this guy. Huge! Well, at least now she could get on that plane and leave without feeling one ounce of…of…

Like a sledgehammer to the face, Fina's anger halted. "Ohmygod. Ohmygod! You just brokenankled me! Didn't you?"

Brutus flashed a glance her way, but didn't re-ply.

"I can't believe you!" she yelled. Now she was really pissed.

"I'm sorry, Fina. I just..."

"What? You just what?" she snapped.

"I know your people need you. I know you're doing what's right for them and for my daughters, but I cannot go with you." His voice was low and riddled with grief.

"Why not?"

He pulled off on the side of the road between two mailboxes. He turned his body to face her. "I can't leave. Not now. Gabrán, our chief, told me last night that he's leaving for Scotland. He said he's too old and too tired to deal with this crap anymore. And now the gods are missing and thousands of immortals have disappeared, many of them leaving behind families and their mates. My own men, whom I've spent centuries fighting side by side with, are coming out of moral-comas after having done very bad things while under the influence of this plague." He inhaled. "I cannot abandon them. They are my family. And this is a crisis."

"Brutus," Fina put her hand on this thigh and spoke softly, "I understand. I do. But there will always be apocalypses and emergencies and missions and wars. And you will always be the man who runs to help, which I love about you. But when do *you* get to live your life? When will it be *your* turn? Because the way I see it, your days and mine are no longer unlimited."

He bobbed his head and stared down at her hand.

She still felt tingles when they touched. Did he?

"I will try to come and visit as soon as I am able," he said. "I promise. But I must try to find out what happened to the gods and the others."

Fina felt her heart busting apart. She might never see him again. He was mortal now, and searching for missing gods would very likely take him to very dangerous places. "You know the most likely place they've gone is…" She didn't want to say the words.

Brutus nodded. "The underworld."

"Yes. And we've all heard the stories." There were many. Mostly from Cimil, but there were records of ghosts, demons, and other immortal creatures that had managed to come back from the underworld. They told stories of hell, of torture, of places so dark and deep no soul was ever right again after being exposed. Then there were the other parts of the underworld that didn't sound so bad— basically, big parties. Orgies. Feasts. But those were tales that came from Cimil. Personally, she didn't believe any of it. In fact, she would bet that Cimil's time in the underworld, conversing with the souls who resided there, was what drove her mad.

"I know. But I must find them and go wherever the clues take me. This world cannot survive without the gods."

"Even if humans don't care about them anymore?"

He nodded. "That alone makes them all the more important."

Fina shook her head. "Humans don't need that band of misfits. I mean, look at their powers. Garage sale hunting? Drumming? Multiplication? Herding bees?"

"It's not about their powers, Fina. It's that they love this world more than any person ever could. They hope when everyone else thinks the game is over. They believe in humans even when humans do not."

Great. So basically, the gods were a bunch of mascots and cheerleaders at a football game. But Fina now understood that Brutus could not leave the helm when there was no one else to take over. He would not abandon his family for his own desires. "Well, if it makes you feel any better, I think I love you more now than ever."

They locked eyes, and he pulled her mouth to his, giving her a soft kiss. "I love you, too. My warrior princess."

"We still have a few minutes, you know." She smiled.

"Ten. Just give me ten. Twenty at the most."

CHAPTER TWENTY-FOUR

By the time they got back to Brutus's house, Fina was already heated from the tip of her toes to the top of her head. She knew she might never see him again. Or maybe she would. Either way, it would be out of her hands, so she needed to make the most of the few precious moments they were given before their lives took different paths.

They burst through the front door and began peeling off each other's clothes, their mouths never parted for long. She loved the way his soft lips moved and how his stubble scraped her chin. It reminded her of him, actually. Rough on the outside and soft and sweet on the inside.

He finished the last button on the shirt she'd borrowed from him and slid it off her shoulders.

"Wow. You have nothing on underneath." His eyes drifted up and down her body.

"Neither did you." She loved that he went commando. It made taking off his pants and shirt so much fun. Instant gratification.

He picked her up and tossed her over his shoulder. "Let's get my little warrior princess to my bed." He smacked her ass.

She yelped. Little? She was almost as tall as him, but whatever.

He tossed her down on the bed and stood there for a long moment.

"What are you waiting for? Clock is ticking," she said.

"I don't know when I'll see you again, and I want to remember this moment."

"Ah." She nodded. "So you can jerk off to me."

"Exactly."

"Then stare away." She opened her legs for him and watched his cock go from thick to a hard solid, throbbing, pulsing missile.

She swallowed down a big lump in her throat. Like she'd said before, Brutus was well proportioned and a big man. But now, looking at the one-eyed beast, she wondered how much fun this would be.

"Do you want me to use a condom?" he asked. "Because I don't have any."

She laughed. "Well then, you're in luck because I'm over three hundred years old."

"Which means?"

"I'm old enough to know what I want, and I'm not letting my sisters all have your kids."

"Are you certain?"

"Yeah. Besides, we pride ourselves on raising tough women. It is our way. It's what we do." Or would do again now that she would be queen and allow men in their village. "Are you okay with that?"

Brutus's big chest expanded as he inhaled. "I

am. In fact, I feel honored you'd even consider it."

How sweet.

He crawled toward her on the bed, settling between her thighs but keeping his weight off her with his arms.

"Are you ready? Do you want me to go down on you first or warm you up or—just tell me what you want."

She pressed her hand to his rough cheek. "I want you inside me. Now. And I want you to kiss me."

He lowered his head and covered her mouth, his tongue massaging and thrusting in a sexual rhythm. She felt him position the head of his cock at her entrance, teasing her with it, dipping it in and out just a little.

Oh wow. That feels so good. Her nipples beaded. Her clit throbbed with a delicious ache. The wall of her—

Brutus pushed inside.

Ouch! Ouch! Ouch! She clenched her eyes shut and dug her nails into his upper arms.

"Are you all right?" he asked. "You said *now*, and I thought—"

"Yeah. Yeah. Yeah. Just, uh…give me a sec." *Wow.* Mortal bodies were so much more sensitive. She honestly hadn't taken that into account!

He brushed the hair from her face and kissed her forehead. "Just tell me when."

The stinging sensation began to subside, replaced by a more pleasant tingling. It was strange how she could feel him filling her, stretching her, but the more intense sensation was in the front, on her clit, and toward the little spot near her womb.

Instinctively, she began moving her hips, enjoying the sensation of his cock pushing against both spots.

"Mmmm…" he groaned into her neck, finding her hands and pressing them over her head. "You're ready for more, I can tell."

Oh yeah. And to think, her mother wanted to deprive her of this? For basically her entire life? No way.

Brutus pulled out almost completely and slowly guided himself back in between her slick folds. This time, the penetration felt amazing. Sinful even.

She moaned. "Do that again. Please."

He did. Nice and slow, allowing her to feel him enter and enjoy the delicious ache of being filled again. Every stroke brought another, deeper, more intense reaction from her body.

He ran his hand down to her breast and gently squeezed her nipple. It triggered an entirely new sensation deep in her womb. Then his mouth went to her neck. He sucked and massaged a sensitive spot that almost tickled.

Oh gods. This is incredible. Whatever was happening right now, she was at the mercy of his pistoning hips, his huge thick dick, and his mouth and hands. Every nerve ending inside her body felt like it was lighting up and glowing, wanting to explode in a blazing light of ecstasy-filled fireworks.

"I think I'm about to..." Her breathing got harder. "To...to..."

Brutus pulled out again and slammed home, pressing his cock as deeply as possible, triggering the release.

Yes! Yes! Yes! were the only thoughts her mind could form as the hard wave of orgasmic contractions took hold. Her toes curled and she moaned, raising her hips to meet his. All of these things were subconsciously done, her mind vaguely aware that her body was in control.

Just as she thought that the pleasure couldn't possibly get more intense, Brutus let out a deep, animalistic groan. His hands went for hers again, threading with her fingers as he squeezed.

His release sparked one more sinful contraction deep in her womb. She felt her walls involuntarily flexing around him, milking his cock for every drop of cum.

After a few moments, their two bodies panting and slick with sweat, Brutus let go of her hands, and he dropped his head into the crook of her neck.

"I don't think I've ever come so hard in my entire life," he muttered.

She smiled up at the ceiling. She wanted to say it was good to hear, considering all the women he'd been with in her village, but why ruin the moment? *Still, if he ever does come to visit, I am so tying him to that tree to have my way with him.*

"I'm going to miss you, Fina," he whispered against her goosebump-covered neck.

Suddenly, her afterglow vanished, and hard reality kicked her in the gut. She would miss him, too. More than words could express. "Then don't be long."

"I won't. I promise."

CHAPTER TWENTY-FIVE

Seeing Fina off that morning was quite possibly the hardest thing Brutus had ever done. Harder than fighting a rabid pack of well-trained sifting vampires possessed by dark magic. Harder than having to watch Cimil tango in the nude with a banana in her butthole. *Very disturbing.* But she really got into her holidays, and since international prostate awareness day and international banana day both fell on April 15, she'd decided to combine the two holidays. Anyway, leaving Fina was harder than that, which said a lot.

He had kissed her up until the very last minute and promised to come to her just as soon as he could. She promised to call him if anything went south with her mother and the coup. All he could do now was pray. To whom? He didn't know. The gods were all missing, and he doubted they could hear him, wherever they'd gone.

Brutus spent the rest of the day gathering information from the remaining men. All in all, only ten percent of the immortals had survived, but those individuals were now human. The human Uchben soldiers were all but wiped out. Their doctors, lawyers, and teachers—anyone who had not been on the front lines—were in good shape and stepping in to assist where possible. But, basically, the entire infrastructure the gods had built in order to assist humans at the drop of a hat was now a skeleton crew. At their own location, in Sedona, they had just under a hundred people.

Brutus went into the chief's office to find out when he planned to leave, but instead found a note. Gabrán must've left that morning. *He didn't even say goodbye in person?* After everything they'd been through together, it was shocking.

> *Brutus:*
>
> *I am sorry, lad, to leave you like this, but I must. I have spent over six hundred years running from battle to battle, disaster to disaster, and all I have to show for it is a wee parcel of land and a pile of old stones that was once my family's great castle. And now, I am out of time, with only forty or so good years left in me. I wish you all the luck in the world, my brother. But do not make the same mistake I did. Do not waste your entire life trying, wishing, and fighting to make the world perfect. 'Tis nay going to come. So let the younger ones pay their dues. Us old warriors deserve to find some peace.*
>
> *Now piss off and get back to work!*
> *—Gabrán*

Brutus folded up the letter and shoved it into his pocket. Perhaps Gabrán was right. Perhaps it was time to shut it all down—the Uchben, their bases, the satellites, submarine factory, nuclear power plants, immortal roller rink, exotic creature petting zoo, and even the Randy Unicorn—the nightclub run by Forgetty and Belch. The gods had spent countless centuries building armies and infrastructure, doing everything in their power to keep humans safe from evil, only to land here with a Universe that kicked them out and humans who no longer believed in them. *Hashtags and memes are the new gods now.*

Yes, it was time to let go. Time to live his life and let the world, let mankind decide for itself what it truly wanted. If the Universe wanted the gods and other immortals to return, she would make it happen.

Brutus walked out into the control center, looking around the room at all of the mates who'd been left behind and had come to help—Emma, Ashli, Margarita, Rys (asshole), Roberto, Sadie, Penelope, Távas, Charlotte, Antonio, Margaret, and Tula. Then there were his men, his brothers, whom he greatly respected.

Brutus went to the front of the room and cleared his throat.

"Everyone, I want you all to know how much you have meant to me, but I have an announcement..."

৵৵ ৵৵

Fina thought the return to the village had gone fairly smoothly. The group of ninety-four women, including herself, showed up and told the queen her reign was over. The queen and her five minions decided to jump into the pit of hellfire and die in "honor."

No one stopped them.

Fina had to wonder, though. Why had her mother been so heartless and cruel? She didn't seem to care about anyone or anything except her own power. That and terrorizing everyone to get what she wanted. In any case, the only sorrow Fina felt now was that her mother had thrown away a chance to be something more than an unloved queen. She could have been a real mother. And a grandmother.

Fina gazed into the bonfire and rested her hand on her belly.

Yes, Brutus had given her a wonderful gift, and now all the remaining women in the tribe would be having little warrior girls to carry on a new tradition. They would be pushed to expand their minds and know that no matter what, they were strong, they were loved.

"Hey, Fina. It's for you!" One of her sisters came up and handed Fina the sat phone. Brutus had insisted she take it along with a solar-powered charger.

"Hello?"

"Hey, warrior princess."

Brutus. The deep sound of his voice filled her heart. "Long time no talk, mister. And it's warrior queen now—or as I like to call myself, benevolent ruler."

"It's only been a month. And you'll always be Princess Fina to me—the woman who first saved my body and then saved my soul."

She swooned on the inside, but held it in. She didn't want to appear all gushy and weak around the others, who were surely eavesdropping from over in the grilling hut. They were having fish tonight. It made her think of Brutus. Because he'd caught her a fish that one time.

"Well, keep saying nice things and see where it gets you, warrior boy." She smiled.

"I'm hoping it'll get me in your pants."

Fina suddenly noticed that the voice hadn't come through the phone. She turned her head and found Brutus with a baby carrier strapped to his chest. The tiny furry faces of Señor Gato and Niccolo were peeking out.

Oh gods. So cute. It made her heart ache. The rest of him made her everything else ache.

She stared for a long moment and then... "Screw it! I don't care if they see me gushing." She ran and threw her arms around his neck, careful not to squish the furbabies. She pressed her lips to his. "I missed you!"

"And I missed you." He banded a strong arm

around her waist and kissed her again.

Little snickers and awwws broke out from the communal hut.

"Hello, ladies," Brutus called out to the women. "How are we all feeling?"

Fina released her grip and helped Brutus off with his BabyBjorn.

"I brought everyone crackers and chocolate. I wasn't sure what you'd like." He pulled the pack from his back and set it on the ground.

"I'll take that. Thank you!" Chela swooped by and disappeared into a ravenous mob of pregnant women.

"That was nice of you." Fina smiled at her big strong guy. She still hadn't broken the news to Brutus that he was going to be a father. Again.

"I have arranged to have more supplies dropped in a few days—food, cloth diapers, biodegradable soap, medicine, a satellite TV, satellite comm system and laptops so the girls have internet for their education, and some construction materials. Seriously, your huts suck, and I really object to my daughters getting rained on."

"Brutus, you must've spent a fortune."

"Eh, well, I sold my house, and the twenty acres of land in Sedona next to it went for top dollar. Plus, I've been saving money for a really, really long time."

It's funny. She had no idea how old Brutus was. *Maybe it's better I don't ask.* She liked thinking of him as her younger man. Wouldn't want to burst that bubble.

"Any update on the missing immortals?" she asked.

"No. But I decided to hand the mission off. I'm done with being a soldier."

"Really?" Fina felt her heart squeeze inside her chest. "So…you're staying? For good?"

"Yes."

There were no words. Saying she felt happy simply didn't cut it. "What made you change your mind?" she asked, knowing how important his work was to him.

"I realized that waiting for the world to be perfect in order to start enjoying my life and finding happiness was pretty stupid. Especially now."

"Because you're no longer immortal?" she asked.

"No, because I have you."

Fina's stomach rolled, but in a good way. She felt like she'd walked into a romantic dream. *And I never want to wake up.* Her life was officially perfect. And hard. With memories of dark moments. And regrets. But she was starting to learn there was a divine wisdom to it all. Bad things and people made the good more valuable. Like now, for example. Not being possessed by evil was really wonderful. Not wanting to slit everyone's throats wasn't bad either.

"As long as this is really what *you* want," she said, "and you won't feel guilty about not running around, saving the world."

"I made my peace with it. And funnily enough, the moment I stepped down, some of the gods' mates started coming up with a plan to get the gods back."

"You think they'll figure out a way?" Honestly, Fina felt for them. To be left so suddenly must be horrible. To not know what happened or where they were would be a nightmare.

"I don't know," Brutus replied. "They'll need someone really smart, someone very brave, and someone who knows something about the under-world—if that is, in fact, where they are."

Who knew? "Well," Fina flashed a bright smile, "let's not think about that for now. This is a happy moment, and you and I need to celebrate. There's this really nice tree over the hill that has been missing you."

Brutus's blue eyes flickered with annoyance.

"Sorry. Sorry. *Mea culpa.* My hut works great, too. Plus, I have something to show you." Still cradling the pets in her arms, she turned and urged him to follow. She opened the bamboo door to her hut and let him enter first.

"Is that..." Brutus pointed to the little pair of pink baby boots on her bed. One of the women knew how to knit and had been teaching her.

"Yep." Fina set the kitten and dog down on the bed and picked up the booties, placing them on her stomach. "How do you think they'll look?"

"Seriously?" Brutus's eyes lit up. It was the exact

same look he'd had that time he looked at Colel when she found the two of them in the jungle. Fina remembered wishing that a man, him specifically, would one day look at her like that.

And now he was. Only this time, his entire face lit up, not just the eyes. He stood a little taller, prouder, and fiercer, too. Yes, he would do anything to protect her and their love.

Even better, he's going to have lots of sex with me and fix the damned roof!

CHAPTER TWENTY-SIX

Nine months later…

Brutus had never sweat so much. He was dripping from head to toe, pacing from one end of the village to the other, then hiking up to the waterfall and down again. Anything to stop worrying.

All ninety-four women, who not only had their moon cycles together for the last five centuries but also decided to go into labor together too, were about to give birth.

The only consolation was that forty of the men in his old platoon, including the small elite group of soldiers with whom he used to have a telepathic connection, had come to settle upstream in their own little village. It had been Brutus's suggestion—fine, fine. He'd begged them—given how short-handed he was. Caring for almost a hundred hormonal pregnant females was more work than he could handle.

Also, they were not shy about their sexual needs. The final straw had been when they took him from Fina's hut in the middle of the night and tied him up. Yes. Again! Only, this time, out of loyalty for their new queen, they didn't touch him. They just put toothpicks in his eyelids and made him watch as they touched themselves.

Brutus cringed. *I can't believe these pervy women are going to mother my children.* Fina had laughed it off and said it was actually pretty nice of them, since they hadn't actually broken any rules.

Anyway, he thought it was wise to bring in reinforcements, and after hundreds of years of saving asses, the men owed him a few favors. Now, there were more men to help fetch snacks and water. The men had more sex and hot women than they knew what to do with.

"Brutus! Brutus!" Fina screamed.

Oh gods. It's time. He ran to the hut and spoke outside the door. "Can I come in now? Is it safe?" Fina had thrown a dagger at him about an hour ago and told him to jump in the crevasse to be with her mother.

"Yes! Safe! Come here!" she screamed.

Brutus poked his head inside, only to see Fina…well, squeezing out a baby. "Wow. Now that is incredible!"

"Shut up! Only you would think that! Get over here and get ready to catch it."

Brutus was about to tell her how beautiful she looked bringing a new life into the world, but the moment he opened his mouth, the little thing was halfway out. He grabbed the clean blanket to her side and caught the little devil just as it popped out.

"Great job!" Brutus looked at the most beautiful creature, besides the mother, he'd ever seen. "Wait. Why does it have a penis? Is that normal for girls?"

"What?" Fina screamed. "No!"

"Yes!" He puffed out his chest and wrapped his little soldier in his arms. "Hello, Señor Baby. It's *very* nice to meet you!"

Fina gave Brutus a dirty look. "Over my dead body will that be his name."

Suddenly, Brutus heard hysterical screams throughout the village. "Then I guess you'd all better start coming up with really great boy names." Brutus could not wish for more in life—his new life. For centuries, he'd given up so much, and it seemed that now the Universe was paying him back in spades. A good woman who loved him and an entire village of sons and warriors. Life couldn't possibly get any better.

☙ ❧

Tula was finally at the end of her rope. She'd followed every lead, every translated glyph, and every stupid fairy tale. She'd racked her brain for clues from the hundreds of conversations she'd had with Cimil, and when that didn't pan out, Tula racked every post-immortal being's brains, too.

No one, not even Roberto, who missed Cimil like a sailor misses the sound of the ocean, could come up with a plausible explanation as to where

Zac had gone. Not that she didn't care about the others. She did. She truly did. But her heart didn't ache for them. It ached for the god with a shiny dark mane, tight black leather pants, and eyes that made her soul weep. She'd gotten her body back, he'd made love to her, but this could not be the end of their story.

I won't allow it!

Tula slung her backpack over her shoulder and trudged through Tolmachevo Airport toward the taxi stand. This was the last lead she had—a story from an old Russian song about a Siberian fur trader who came across a magical nymph that…well, basically had her way with him.

From what she knew, nymphs were really sex fairies who'd been caught during their nightly swims. They liked to bathe. A lot. They liked sex a lot, too. Obviously.

Tula pulled up the zipper on her thick black parka and stepped outside to await her ride. Long gone were her frilly dresses and granny panties. Now she went commando, and her clothing was meant for two things: protection from the elements and hiding weapons. A girl like her could hardly go to the most remote, war-torn regions of the world wearing a Gunne Sax. Today, it was snow boots. Yesterday, biker boots. Leather pants, then snow pants. Anything but muumuus.

The blue SUV pulled up, and she hopped in back. "Hi, Yuri. How's it hanging?"

"Goot. Goot. How wuz chor flight?"

"Boring. But at least I got some sleep. Got the gear I asked for?"

"Jesss. And I even found you the 3295 Lugar."

"In pink?" she asked.

"Jesss, ma'am."

"Thank you. You know how I love to feel feminine when I'm trying not to be murdered by drug lords or gangs." Seriously, if Zac knew what she'd gone through just on a hope and a prayer it might lead to him, he'd be kissing her toes for all eternity.

I just hope he's okay... She vaguely remembered the underworld—the place souls went when their turn was over in this world—and from what she could recall, it was a horrible place. Luckily for her, she'd been bound to a deity, bound to this world. That anchor had given her a way back.

"So, are you ready?" Yuri asked.

"As ready as I'll ever be." She'd heard that this particular spot, where the Siberian permafrost was melting, had been turning up all sorts of things. Things not of this world and of worlds that had long passed—dinosaurs, alien ships, and microorganisms. The Russian government did its best to suppress the info, but even they couldn't stop the chatter on the dark web. The latest rumble was that a portal had been found. To the underworld.

Gods, I hope so! She was tired and missed Zac. She didn't know how much longer she could go on.

She pulled out her phone and started checking messages. *Oh. Wow!* Brutus had posted pics of his new sons on Facebook. *Wow. And ninety-four of them. Go, Brutus!*

Suddenly, a text popped onto the screen.

She tapped the box to read the entire message.

Unknown: *I understand you're on your way to visit me. As a courtesy to Cimil, who has been a loyal business partner, I am giving you one chance to turn back.*

What the hell?

Tula: *Who is this?*

Unknown: *Why don't you come and find out?*

Tula: *You just told me to turn back.*

Unknown: *So I did.*

Tula: *How do I know if I should take you seriously if I don't know who you are?*

Unknown: *Because I have your precious god.*

Tula: *Oh really? Then send proof.*

The three dots wiggled on her screen and then a picture popped up. Tula gasped. *Zac?* In all her travels, in all the horror stories she'd read, she'd never seen anything so terrible, so heartbreaking. It was worse than her worst nightmare. It was all her fears magnified by a thousand, with a cherry on top.

Tula: *What do you want?*

Unknown: *See you soon, Tula.*

TO BE CONTINUED…
(But keep reading for good news!)

AUTHOR'S NOTE

Yep! I went there!! But only because you wonderfully crazy people asked for it, and you *know* how tight Cliffy and I are. Inseparable, the two of us. LOL.

The book entitled **ZAC** will be the next installment of the Immortal Matchmakers, Inc. series. WOOHOO!!!

I haven't decided if it will be a novella or full-length novel, but I think you guys were so, so right! The ending of the gods', Zac's, and Tula's journeys are too complicated and FUN to squeeze into this one book. It just felt too busy when I tried. And trust me, I did! For three weeks. But everything I envisioned didn't sit right.

Maybe because I started my writing career with these gods in the Accidentally Yours series, and they've become like family. It seems only befitting to give these insane immortals a very spunky and entertaining send-off.

So, as I'm sure all you smarty-pants noticed in this book, the finale is now set to go! So get ready for one more round! Coming 2021! We'll find out what the deal was with Minky and Mittens, where the immortals went, and who was texting Tula.

In the meantime, please feel free to send me hate mail. I can take it. *Hides under desk in fetal position.* You can also say nice things and ask for a SIGNED *BRUTUS* BOOKMARK! (OMG. LOL! Check out Señor Gato.)

STEP ONE: Email me at Mimi@mimijean.net

STEP TWO: Provide your neat and complete shipping info.

STEP THREE: If you wrote a review for *BRUTUS* because you loved it more than warm chocolate chip cookies, be sure to provide a link or screenshot. I will do my very best to include extra goodies. I always warn readers that I do run out! It's first ask, first get!

STEP FOUR: Give me about 3–4 weeks. I know…I know…it's terrible, but I promise you guys the whole swag mail-out thing has become "a thing." It's an all-day event that requires my assistant, me, and my kids when I can bribe them to stuff envelopes. Still, I LOVE doing it for you guys. In this world of ebooks, it's wonderful to receive something you can touch and hold with the cover on it!

Okay, my immortal warrior princesses and princes! Be sure to sign up for my sorta kinda monthly newsletter. So many fun books on the way! *THE LIBRARIAN'S VAMPIRE ASSISTANT (#5)*, *FANGED LOVE* (Oh yeah! Mr. Nice's Favorite Book), *THE DEAD KING (King #6)*, and *ZAC*.

SIGN UP HERE → www.mimijean.net

With Immortal Hugs,
Mimi

P.S. Brutus Playlist! Hit it here on Spotify!
P.P.S. Brutus on Pinterest.
www.pinterest.com/mimijeanromance/brutus

ACKNOWLEDGMENTS

My undying gratitude to the team of people who support my crazy books and make them happen! Su, Dali, Stephanie, Pauline, and Paul.

To my super cool dudes, who know just what to say to make me laugh when I need it most.

A special shout-out to my readers who've supported this series for years! Wow! Are you guys gluttons for punishment. Are you sure your brains aren't fried by now? LOL!

Also, thanks to Hannah Roberson for supplying the alternate name for Zeus! Señor Gato was perfect for this Mayan-inspired series.

Thank you to Melissa Stigliano Norton for naming Brutus's penis! LOL!!! The General…hehehe…

Finally, thank you to the Mimi Jean Junkies for all of the wonderful ideas pertaining to what sort of creature Minky's mate should be. Seriously awesome! But I bet you're all kicking yourselves now because you don't get to find out what/who Mittens really is until we get to *ZAC*.

All my love,
Mimi

Character Definitions – The Gods

Although every culture around the world has their own names and beliefs related to beings of worship, there are actually only fourteen gods. And since the gods are able to access the human world only through the portals called cenotes, located in the Yucatán, the Mayans were big fans.

Acan—God of Wine and Intoxication, and God of Decapitation. Also known as Belch, Acan has been drunk for many millennia. He generally wears only tighty whities, but since he's the life of the party, he's been known to mix it up and go naked, too. Whatever works. He is now mated to the lovely Margarita.

Ah-Ciliz—God of Solar Eclipses: Called A.C. by his brethren, Ah-Ciliz is generally thought of as a giant buzz kill because of his dark attitude.

Akna—Goddess of Fertility: She is so powerful, it is said she can make inanimate objects fornicate and that anyone who gets in the same room as her ends up pregnant. She is often seen hanging out with her brother Acan at parties, when not hiding in a cave.

Backlum Chaam—God of Male Virility: He was once a slave to the Maaskab and played a key role in discovering that black jade can be used to procreate with humans.

Camaxtli—Goddess of the Hunt: Also once known as Fate until she was discovered to be a fake and had her powers stripped away by the Universe. She's now referred to as "Fake."

Colel Cab—Mistress of Bees: Though she has many, many powers, "Bees" is most known for the live beehive hat on her head. She is now mated to Rys, the florist.

Goddess of Forgetfulness—Also known as Forgetty, she once had no official name because no one could remember it. Now she's mated to Távas and goes by Aurora. When she's not out eating chicken wings at his new restaurant, she spends her evenings DJing at the Randy Unicorn, her nightclub.

Ixtab—Goddess of Happiness (ex-Goddess of Suicide): Ixtab's once morbid frock used to make children scream. But since finding her soul mate, she's now the epitome of all things happy.

K'ak (Pronounced "cock")—The history books remember him as K'ak Tiliw Chan Yopaat, ruler of Copán in the 700s AD. King K'ak is one of Cimil's favorite brothers. We're not really sure what he does, but he can throw bolts of lightning, wears a giant silver and jade headdress with intertwining serpents, and has long black and silver hair.

Kinich Ahau—ex-God of the Sun: Known by many other names, depending on the culture, Kinich likes to go by Nick these days. He's also now a vampire—something he's actually not so bummed about. He is mated to the love of his life, Penelope, the Ruler of the House of Gods.

Máax—Once known as the God of Truth, Máax was banished for repeatedly violating the ban on time travel. However, since helping to save the world from the big "over," he is now known as the God of Time Travel. Also turns out he was the God of Love, but no one figured that out until his mate, Ashli, inherited his power. Ashli is now the fourteenth deity, taking the place of Camaxtli, the Fake.

Votan—God of Death and War: Also known as Odin, Wotan, Wodan, God of Drums (he has no idea how the hell he got that title; he hates drums), and Lord of Multiplication (okay, he is pretty darn good at math so that one makes sense). These days, Votan goes by Guy Santiago (it's a long story—read *ACCIDENTALLY IN LOVE WITH…A GOD?*), but despite his deadly tendencies, he's all heart.

Yum Cimil—Goddess of the Underworld: Also known as Ah-Puch by the Mayans, Mictlantecuhtli (try saying that one ten times) by the Aztec, Grim Reaper by the Europeans, Hades by the Greeks...you get the picture! Despite what people say, Cimil is actually a female, adores a good bargain (especially garage sales) and the color pink, and she hates clowns. She's also bat-shit crazy, has an invisible pet unicorn named Minky, and is married to Roberto, the king of all vampires.

Zac Cimi—Once thought to be the God of Love, we now know differently. Zac is the God of Temptation, and his tempting ways have landed him in very hot water. Because no matter how temptingly hot your brother's mate might be, trying to steal her is wrong. He is currently serving time for his crime in Los Angeles with Cimil, running the Immortal Matchmakers agency. He is now madly in love with his assistant, Tula.

Character Definitions –
Not the Gods

Andrus: Ex-Demilord (vampire who's been given the gods' light), now just a demigod after his maker, the vampire queen, died. He is now happily mated to Sadie, a half-succubus who spends her days feeding off of her delicious new hubby and going to casting calls in LA.

Ashli: Ashli actually belongs over in the GODS section, but since she was born human, we'll keep her here. Ashli is mate to Máax, God of Time Travel. Unbeknownst to him, he was also the God of Love. Ashli inherited his power after they started falling in love. Maybe the Universe thought a woman should have this power?

Brutus: One of the gods' elite Uchben warriors. He doesn't speak much, but that's because he and his team are telepathic. They are also immortal (a gift from the gods) and next in line to be Uchben chiefs.

Charlotte: Sadie's golf-loving half-sister and the intended mate to Andrus Grey. Only, Andrus, being the rebel that he is, decided he could pick his own damned woman, Sadie. Charlotte is now happily mated to Tommaso, Andrus's BBF. They're one big happy family! Oh, and her daddy is an incubus.

Helena Strauss: Once human, Helena is now a vampire and married to Niccolo DiConti. She has a half-vampire daughter, Matty, who is destined to marry Andrus's son, according to Cimil.

Margarita Seville: Once a member of the Amish community, Margarita now lives in LA, following her calling to make the world a healthier place. She owns a successful gym and has a teenage daughter, Jessica, who's hell-bent on making her life miserable. She is mate to Acan, God of Wine.

Matty: The infant daughter of Helena and Niccolo, destined to marry Andrus's son.

Niccolo DiConti: General of the Vampire Army. Now that the vampire queen is dead, the army remains loyal to him. He shares power with his wife, Helena Strauss, and has a half-vampire daughter, Matty.

Penelope: Part angel and part human, Penelope is mated to Kinich. When he turned into a vampire, she inherited his sun god powers and became the Ruler of the House of Gods.

Reyna: The dead vampire queen.

Roberto (Narmer): Originally an Egyptian pharaoh, Narmer was one of the six Ancient Ones—the very first vampires. He eventually changed his name to Roberto and moved to Spain—something to do with one of Cimil's little schemes. He now spends his days lovingly undoing Cimil's treachery, being a stay-at-home dad, and taking her unicorn Minky for a ride.

Rys: Mate to Colel. He was allergic to bees and got stung, so Colel's vampire brother had to save him. Colel gifted Rys the light of the gods and made him a demilord so now he's just a big, bad, powerful immortal florist.

Sadie: Charlotte's half-sister and mated to Andrus Grey, Sadie is an aspiring actress who discovered she's also half succubus.

Távas: Once the king of the Maaskab who lived for killing and making thumb necklaces, he is now mated to Forgetty and has decided to modernize his evil ways. His first business venture is opening a chain of chicken wing restaurants. After that, he plans to go into video game production.

Tommaso: Once a soldier of the gods, called Uchben, Tommaso's mind was poisoned with black jade. He tried to kill Emma, Votan's mate, but redeemed himself by turning into a spy for the gods. He is now mated to Charlotte.

Tula: The incorruptible administrative assistant at Immortal Matchmakers, Inc.

ABOUT THE AUTHOR

MIMI JEAN PAMFILOFF is a *New York Times* bestselling author who's sold over one million books around the world. Although she obtained her MBA and worked for more than fifteen years in the corporate world, she believes that it's never too late to come out of the romance closet and follow your dreams.

Mimi lives with her Latin lover hubby, two pirates-in-training (their boys), and their three spunky dragons (really, just very tiny dogs with big attitudes) Snowy, Mini, and Mack, in the vampire-unfriendly state of Arizona.

She hopes to make you laugh when you need it most and continues to pray daily that leather pants will make a big comeback for men.

Sign up for Mimi's mailing list for giveaways and new release news!